# IN TOO DEEP

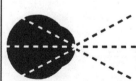
This Large Print Book carries the
Seal of Approval of N.A.V.H.

# IN TOO DEEP

## STACEY WEEKS

**THORNDIKE PRESS**

A part of Gale, a Cengage Company

Farmington Hills, Mich • San Francisco • New York • Waterville, Maine
Meriden, Conn • Mason, Ohio • Chicago

Thorndike Press, a part of Gale, a Cengage Company.

Thorndike Press® Large Print Christian Mystery.
The text of this Large Print edition is unabridged.
Other aspects of the book may vary from the original edition.
Set in 16 pt. Plantin.

**LIBRARY OF CONGRESS CIP DATA ON FILE.**
**CATALOGUING IN PUBLICATION FOR THIS BOOK**
**IS AVAILABLE FROM THE LIBRARY OF CONGRESS**

ISBN-13: 978-1-4328-6161-2 (hardcover)

Published in 2019 by arrangement with White Rose Publishing, a division of Pelican Ventures, LLC

Printed in Mexico
1 2 3 4 5 6 7 23 22 21 20 19

Dedicated to God my Father.
May I always take seriously the
responsibility that comes with
proclaiming God's truth.
Thank you to my family for
giving me the freedom to follow
my passion to write.
Special thanks to Jane Hart for
the idea that plugged a plot hole
and to Jean Miller for the name
Camp Moshe, which means to
pull/draw out of the water.
Much thanks to fellow writer and
friend Sandra Orchard, without
your help and input, I would have
given up long ago.

# 1

Kye Campton shrugged out of his dark suit coat and tossed it through the open window of his two-door sedan parked in front of Camp Moshe's offices. He had some time to kill before meeting with the camp's new swim instructor, Grace Stone. He folded up the cuffs of his suit pants, unbuttoned the top three buttons of his white dress shirt, and walked barefoot toward the sandy shoreline of Lake Moshe. The lapping coolness of the Georgian Bay washed over his toes, and he inhaled June's promise of heat.

A small boy paddled a blue canoe, and a smile tugged at his lips. If he had his way — and he usually did — this place would be crawling with kids canoeing, parasailing, horseback riding, and enjoying God's creation. The peaceful backdrop of the sun peeking over the swelling hilltops would draw families in need of rest. Which, according to his doctor, also happened to be what he needed. He was set to collide with burnout, and thirty-year-olds shouldn't get burnout.

"Look out!" A blur of red streaked past him, knocking him to his hands and knees. Water sprayed out around him.

"Hey!" He pushed up and shook off the wet.

The girl's sweater hit the sand as she sacrificed a quick glance back, her dark hair billowing out around her head. "Call 911!"

911? His eyes snapped to the horizon. Waves lapped against the side of a capsized canoe. The boy! A crest of water washed over a small form and pushed it underneath the rolling surface. Kye fumbled for his phone and rushed knee-deep into the lake while punching in the numbers.

Pounding feet on the nearby dock dragged his gaze to the left. The woman had stripped down to a bathing suit and shouted indecipherable commands into the wind. The breeze snatched her words away. Before he could shout, move, or do anything, she dove into the lake.

An authoritative voice sounded from his phone. "911, how may I direct your call?"

"We need an ambulance at Camp Moshe." He glanced around, searching for the nearest lifeguard tower. "We are at the beach front by tower number two. A child is in trouble in the lake . . . Yes, someone has gone in after him. She's . . . she's . . ." he tracked her movements. Her toned arms cleanly sliced through the water with confident strokes and, despite swimming against the current, her pace never slowed. "She doesn't seem to be struggling. She's got the boy now. She's pulling him in." She exhibited impressive strength and competence as she turned the boy over, tucked him into the crook of her arm while supporting his head, and swam him in.

The operator wanted him to stay on the line. He punched the speaker option and slipped the phone into his shirt pocket. He waded deeper into the water meeting her at hip level. He wordlessly took the still child from her arms. She must be tired, although she didn't look it. He carried the boy to the beach and lay him down on the sand. Before he even had a chance to look him over, she nudged him out of the way.

"Is he breathing?" The operator's voice blasted through his phone.

Kye snatched it out of his pocket. "I think so."

The woman checked the boy's airway and monitored his chest. Seemingly satisfied with what she saw, she rolled him onto his side and extended one arm out perpendicular to his body and pulled up one knee into his chest. The child spluttered and coughed.

"That's right." The woman rubbed his back in comforting, circular motions. "Cough it out."

Her velvety voice slowed Kye's panic and seemed to calm the child who only looked about eight years old. He seemed old enough to know better than to go out on the lake alone, but young enough to make reckless decisions.

She sat back on her heels, never shifting her eyes from the boy's face. Her damp hair hung down her back in tangled waves and clung to her tanned skin. Her strong physique, muscled but still feminine, hardly seemed winded; but then he noticed the slight heaving of her chest. Her sharp and silent intake of oxygen belied her facade of ease.

He turned off speakerphone and spoke directly into the mouthpiece. "I hear the sirens. The ambulance is almost here and the boy is coughing. He seems to be OK. Thank you." Kye disconnected.

He met the woman's eyes. If she hadn't been here . . . "Thank you."

Paramedics dropped down beside the boy, and she gave them a succinct summary of events while stepping back to give them the space they needed to work.

He waited for her attention. Nothing. She fixated on the child at first, and then her eyes closed and her lips moved. Was she praying? He cleared his throat.

Finally, she looked at him. In the brief second they made visual contact, fear, relief, and exhaustion flashed through her eyes.

"Thank you," he tried again.

"You're welcome."

He waited for her to say more, but she didn't. Instead, she shaded her eyes and studied Camp Moshe's boatshed. After a few seconds, she shifted her interest to the empty lifeguard tower and finally rested on the camp offices just up the gravel path where he had parked his car. Her eyes narrowed before they swung back to him and roamed up and down the length of his body. He got the feeling that both he and the camp had failed some sort of test.

"Why wasn't the boatshed locked? Camp Moshe always locks their boatshed until the lifeguards start work at the end of June. Where's Uncle Carl? Who'd he leave in charge of the beach?" She fired her questions one after the other.

Kye blinked. She knew too much about camp to be a cottager on vacation. The only person scheduled to be here right now, who'd dive into the lake without hesitation and ask these kinds of questions with such authority, was Grace Stone. This was not the way he had planned to meet his predecessor's niece.

Before he could respond, she whipped around and her wet hair slapped against her cheek. She started back toward the dock, scooping up her discarded sweater as she went, mumbling something that sounded like, "Never mind. I'll find out for myself what sort of clown is running this place."

Kye knew he should have let her walk away. But against his better judgment, he followed at a respectful distance, comparing her to the polished women he usually rubbed shoulders with in the business world. She radiated simplicity, like the girl next door but all grown up. She'd probably choose jeans, flip-flops, and a beach BBQ over dining at a splashy, high-end restaurant. He'd bet she was nothing like his high maintenance ex-fiancé, Annette.

She gathered the rest of her discarded clothing and paused at the end of the dock, looking out over the water. The morning sun glowed, creating a tranquil, almost postcard-like, picture.

Kye waited. She had to come back this

way at some point. She finally turned. If she was surprised to see him standing there, she hid it well. She walked toward him, appearing neither repentant for her earlier onslaught of questions nor embarrassed by them.

Kye blocked her path with an extended hand before she could brush past him. "Kye Campton. Interim Camp Director." He met her widened eyes and lifted one brow before wryly adding, "The clown in charge."

Grace blinked.

This guy was in charge of the beach? She flicked her eyes down his length again. Somehow he seemed better suited for office work.

She needed to find Uncle Carl. She couldn't imagine him hiring some bozo incapable of keeping the boatshed locked until the lifeguards arrived. There must be a reasonable explanation for placing a businessman in charge of the water. And what in the world did interim mean? Uncle Carl was the camp director.

She took another look at his soggy business slacks and untucked shirt as she accepted his offered hand. His thumb swiped across her knuckles as their gazes held.

Despite her critical perception of him

seconds earlier, her insides swirled like the sandy lake bottom.

He held on a nanosecond longer than necessary, and his warm, firm clasp was not the clammy, limp fish she expected from a displaced office man. An unexpected waft of coconut sunscreen further belied his business attire.

She straightened up. "I'm Grace Stone. Sorry for the clown comment. It wasn't kind or necessary."

He stared at her without saying a word, and she fought the urge to squirm. Shouldn't the director of a Christian camp be quicker to forgive? Besides, if he was in charge, he was responsible for that boat-shed. She had seen from the parking lot that the drowning boy was in a camp boat. All the camp boats were blue and displayed the Camp Moshe logo. How did this guy miss it? She held his stare and lifted her chin. Once Uncle Carl heard about this oversight — and boy would he hear about it — this interim director could kiss his job good-bye.

Kye hitched his head toward the office. "We can meet in my office in about fifteen minutes. I'll need to speak with the paramedics before they leave, and I'll clean up anything they leave on the beach."

"Your office?" she parroted.

"Yes." He pointed to the office buildings as if she wouldn't know where they were.

"I know where the offices are."

"Good, then you won't be late." He flashed a quick grin that displayed one perfect dimple in his left cheek, and she steeled her lurching heart. Even if he was a good guy, launching her water safety program required all her time and attention. She had no interest in diving into the shallow waters of a summer fling.

She nodded, and he trotted off toward the paramedics who were speaking with a distraught couple, presumably the boy's parents. She pulled her loose weave sweater over her head and tugged her jeans up over her hips, thankful she had worn her suit under her clothes. The lake water would soak through in minutes, but it was all she had. She had planned to swim after their meeting, not before.

*What is going on, Lord? This wasn't how I planned my big comeback to Camp Moshe.*

Fifteen minutes later, she stood in Kye's office, formerly Uncle Carl's office, twisting her fingers together and wishing she had dry clothes. Armed with new information gleaned from Judy, the director's administrative assistant, she felt somewhat up to speed. Judy spent the last five minutes alternating between dabbing her eyes over the financial mess sinking the camp and wiping them over Uncle Carl's early, unexpected retirement. She worked her way through an entire package of travel-sized tissues in their brief conversation.

Grace gathered enough information to get the gist. Some first-rate smarty-pants had managed to convince the board of directors that Camp Moshe needed a new, younger face. They bought out Uncle Carl and turned the place upside-down. If the scuttlebutt in the lobby could be believed, Camp Moshe was re-launching as an extreme sports camp — a concept that wasn't just crazy, but downright dangerous. She shuddered. She'd been in enough dangerous situations in her twenty-nine years to last her a lifetime.

Thank the Lord He brought her here to slow down the man hurling Camp Moshe toward disaster. Dangling danger in front of kids was like playing with fire. Children had no concept of their limitations, often overestimating their abilities. Sure, some of it was normal kid stuff, but sometimes things took a deadly, unexpected turn.

*Don't go there.*

She swiped her eyes and stuffed the memories deep. She couldn't go there. Not right now.

"So you're Grace Stone." From behind her, a dry, refreshed-looking Kye strode into the room, yanking her from her thoughts.

"The way you pulled that boy in," Kye's voice momentarily hitched and he swallowed hard. "You're everything your uncle said you were and more."

"Uncle Carl?" Funny that her uncle never mentioned Kye to her.

Kye moved behind his desk and gestured to the armchair on her left. "He said you were a firecracker and a first-rate lifeguard. I wish we could have met under calmer, less life-threatening circumstances, but seeing you in action, well, that was something else. You surpassed even your uncle's description. You're clearly qualified for the position."

"That wasn't an audition." She ignored his gesture to sit. She'd need to employ every trick in the book to maintain the upper hand.

"No," his expression sobered. "But I am thankful you were there." He adjusted his shirt cuff and sat down.

How did he clean up so fast? What did he have, a dozen suits exactly the same style, cut, and color hanging in a storage locker

17

somewhere? She pulled her sweater tighter, even more aware that her jeans and back were now wet through.

"Kye is an interesting name."

He looked surprised at her attempt at small talk. "It's short for Malachi. My mother is very," he paused as if searching for the right word, "fundamental. Your name made me chuckle too."

"Grace?"

"No, Stone. You know, since you're a swim instructor and stones sink?"

She fought the urge to roll her eyes.

He shuffled some papers on his desk and cleared his throat. "Please, sit."

"I'm good, thanks."

He stared for a moment and then shrugged. "Your choice."

"So where is Uncle Carl?" She folded her arms across her chest and pivoted her weight to her right leg. The wet denim stuck to her thigh in the most uncomfortable way. Judy had told her Uncle Carl had retired, but she didn't buy it. Not Uncle Carl. Not without telling her first.

Kye leaned back in his chair and pressed his fingertips together. It made her uncomfortable. "Somewhere in the Caribbean fishing, I believe."

What? She felt behind her for the chair

and sank into the seat. She had made her plans with Uncle Carl and sold her program to him, but she hadn't signed anything. They planned to firm up the details today. How could he leave without telling her? And what did that mean for her program?

"So he's really gone?" She hated the catch in her voice. Uncle Carl was like a father to her and had been since her dad died.

Kye's blue eyes visibly softened as if he had anticipated how she would take this news. "He left two days ago. If it's any consolation, things came together really fast and he tried to call you multiple times, but you were unavailable. He didn't want to email about something this big and thought it was better if I told you when you arrived."

"I had an issue with my cell phone. It was in for repairs."

"He left a forwarding number for you."

He didn't hand it to her. He placed it on the desk and slid it part way across the wooden surface, forcing her to meet him halfway. Likely some sort of smooth business trick learned in school. She gave the paper a cursory glance before closing her eyes. Uncle Carl had mentioned that things were changing at the camp. He said they were good changes, and that he'd fill her in when he could. How could he leave like this? And what was she going to do now? Her program had impressed Uncle Carl, and he booked her for the entire summer — but Uncle Carl wasn't here anymore. He had been replaced by some suit who likely didn't understand the importance of water safety for non-swimmers. He probably believed she was just a glorified lifeguard.

*Lifeguards.* Her eyes snapped opened. "Why was the boatshed unlocked before the lifeguards started? And why wasn't the boy wearing a life jacket?"

Kye shrugged, and his casualness rubbed her raw. "It looks like the kid broke the lock, and it's been my experience that when a kid takes something that doesn't belong to him for a joyride, he's not likely to steal the accompanying safety equipment."

"Does that happen much? Joy-riders? What will you do when they steal rock climbing equipment or paddle boards?" She curled her fingernails into the arms of her chair and willed her voice to remain steady.

He stiffened. Clearly, he didn't expect her to know any camp details. She could almost see the cogs in his brain turning, trying to figure out how she had found out so fast. For once, she felt thankful for Judy's loose tongue. As a thank you, she'd have to buy her one of those specialty coffees she liked

20

so much.

"I don't see how that's any of your concern. But if you don't like the direction I'm steering the camp, you're not obligated to remain as a lifeguard. We don't have a contract." He was testing her. She was sure of it.

"Lifeguard?" She shot to her full five-foot-six-inch frame and towered over the desk. "You have no idea what I do or what plans I made with Uncle Carl. I am not just a lifeguard. I've created a new program geared to help —"

"Non-swimmers survive in the water," he interrupted, patting the air like he wanted her to calm down. "I know. It's called Water Survival for Non-Swimmers. He did tell me. And you'll have a chance to pitch your program to me. Today was supposed to be a get-to-know-you meeting."

It wasn't fair. He knew far more about her than she knew about him. A few well-placed phone calls should fix that.

He tapped his phone and opened an electronic day-planner. "How about two days from now? You could pitch your program to me then." He looked up but didn't stand to reach her level. It was like he couldn't be bothered. Another boardroom trick?

She suddenly felt woozy, and the chair rushed up underneath her. She gratefully sank into it. Would Kye pull the plug? She swallowed her vinegary comeback and replaced it with honeyed words. "I'll be happy to pitch it to you in two days. Uncle Carl and I established a viable plan to recover this camp. This place means a lot to me, and I want to see it succeed." She needed it to succeed. This was her last year to qualify for the young entrepreneurs' grant. And if she wanted this provincial funding, she needed to run the program through a camp.

"Great." Kye shuffled some papers on his desk. "We are on the same page. Turning this place around is my job. It's the whole reason the board of directors turned to my firm for help and contracted me. I am good at my job."

He said it with confidence, but she heard the undertone of a challenge and gobbled the bait. "I'm sure once you hear my pitch, you'll agree with me and Uncle Carl and get on board with our program. Water programs are a safe bet for summer camps. Extreme sports, well, that's a little risky."

His face reddened at the words *safe bet.* "Carl is no longer here, and in case you didn't notice, they called me in to replace him because his 'viable ideas,' " he put air-quotes around the words, "were not attracting campers. Not for the last five years. Camp Moshe is on its last summer unless I can turn this boat around. We are done with safe bets. It's time to take a risk."

"Now you just wait —"

He held up his hand. "Before you get all crazy, Carl was offered a nice severance which he gladly accepted. I did not gun for his job. The board hired me after months of discussion with Carl. They agreed they needed someone with my special skills to save this place. It's what I do."

"But Uncle Carl —"

"Is off on a well-deserved holiday and will be back in the fall to help transition in the new permanent camp director. But for now, you're stuck with me. Like it or not."

She snatched up Uncle Carl's new phone number. Nope, she didn't like it, not one little bit.

# 2

Kye broke from the trees and hit the beach. He slowed just long enough to kick off his shoes and finish his morning jog barefoot. He tried to concentrate on the worship track pulsating through his ear buds, but he couldn't stop thinking about the threatening note he found tacked to his cabin door. Did Grace write it? The idea that she might dislike him enough to threaten him twisted his gut.

He pushed the spirited woman out of his mind and upped his pace until the sand sprayed behind him. It didn't matter. She wouldn't be the first person to try and bully him out of a job. It came with the territory. It had never gone past empty threats in the past.

He veered into the water, and a shock of cold jolted him harder than his 5:00 a.m. coffee. A wave, courtesy of a passing motorboat, lapped over his ankles, shooting numbness up his legs. He angled himself to move higher toward the drier sand on the beach. He dodged pebbles and sticks and made a mental note to arrange for the town to start dragging the sand every morning.

He wrestled with an urge to stop and note that reminder into his phone. He had so many details crammed inside his head he was afraid he'd only remember this task tomorrow morning when the sticks and stones stabbed his feet again.

Before he could decide, his phone vibrated in his armband. He slowed to a brisk walk. Killing two birds with one stone, he made his note and swiped his thumb down the phone's touch screen. Tamera Campton. His mother. He considered letting it go to voicemail — except, did she know about the note? He'd sheltered her from the disgruntled employees he'd dealt with in the past and didn't intend to start including her now. His reputation as a fixer made him popular with the board members and share-holders of struggling corporations but not so much with staff. When someone like him arrived, the following employee overhaul pushed some personalities to the edge.

"Hello?"

"Good morning Malachi. I held dinner

until nine o'clock last night. Were you unwell?"

He'd bailed on dinner last night. This call must be his punishment. He drew a calming breath and stopped. It was too hard to keep up his vigorous pace and keep up with his scheming mother. "I'm fine, Mom. I told you I wouldn't be able to make dinner. Did you forget?" He should have left his phone at home and jogged without the tunes today.

"Sarah was so disappointed you cancelled. It's a shame. She's such a lovely girl." Her displeasure oozed through the connection.

"You never mentioned Sarah." He had suspected her ulterior motive for dinner included a woman. Ever since he had called off his engagement to Annette, his mother repeatedly expressed how she hated his transitory lifestyle that made dating difficult, marriage unlikely, and grandchildren non-existent. For a mother determined to keep him healthy and happy, she seemed oblivious to the effect her Cupid-inspired ploys had on his blood pressure.

"Would you have come if I had told you about her?" Her hopeful tone squashed his frustration. She really did want him to be happy.

"Mom, I'm here to work. This isn't a vacation."

"But the doctor said —"

"I know what the doctor said, Mom," he softened his voice. "I was there. And a holiday won't fix this. Ulcers are caused by bacteria." He never should have told her about his ulcer.

"I don't know. I always heard it was stress. Besides, why would he tell you to slow down and take better care of your health if stress wasn't an issue?" She continued as if he hadn't spoken.

The doctor had also said that his meddling mother wasn't helping things, but he couldn't tell her that, could he? "Stress exacerbates the ulcer, it doesn't cause it, and I am taking care of myself, Mom. In fact, I was just running. For the sake of my health, maybe we should cut this short so I can finish my workout."

"When the doctor recommended that you take some time off, I had hoped you would spend that time with me." Her voice petered off.

He softened. "You're only twenty minutes away. I can come and visit during my down time. That's partly why I took this job. It's almost as good as a holiday." Except dodging her wanna-be-wives wasn't a vacation. It was an exercise in patience that would surely make his ulcer worse, not better, no matter what the doctor said about bacteria.

Just then, Grace Stone padded down a nearby dock in a tattered bathrobe. He wasn't sure which look he liked better. Yesterday's feisty girl in soaked jeans and sweater, or today's softer woman with incredibly cute morning-mussed hair. His stomach lurched.

"Malachi? Are you even listening to me?" His mother's sharp tone reeled him back into the conversation.

"I'm sorry, Mom, I missed that."

"Good morning!" Grace's cheerful greeting skipped across the waves.

Kye waved back and then yanked his hand down to his side. There was something about the way she carried herself, a strange mix of vulnerability and confidence, that he found inviting. She tempted him to mix business with pleasure, but that wasn't his style.

Especially if she was the source of the not-so-subtle intimidation tactics.

"Who was that? Was that a woman?" His mother nattered in his ear.

"It's no one, Mom. Listen, I'd like to take you to dinner tomorrow night. Please let me do this to make up for last night." At least this way he could control the guest list. "My treat, Mom. Please?"

"Fine," she said. "I'll be ready at seven." She agreed too readily. Did she have another trick up her sleeve?

"See you then, Mom. Love you." He swiped down the screen and disconnected just as Grace disrobed and executed a shallow dive that hardly disturbed the water. After a few seconds, her head broke the surface and she cut long, even strokes toward Moshe Island.

"She's got great form, doesn't she?" Graham Douglas chuckled from behind him.

Kye spun around, instantly recalling what he knew about the Douglas family. He had been working on memorizing the names of the locals and the regular seasonal visitors. Especially the financial supporters of Camp Moshe.

"Morning, Graham. Heading out for some fishing?" He dodged the Grace question and nodded at the tackle box and the disposable dish with the word bait scrawled across the front. The Douglas family arrived every summer on the first of June. Mr. Douglas taught at a nearby university, and after he submitted his final grades he scooped up the missus and their boy and hid out here for three months. Their son, Jeremy, was homeschooled, and they arranged his year to finish up around the same time as his father.

"Can't beat fishing from a boat in the middle of a calm lake. You should come out with me some time. Completely relaxing."

"Hmm?" Kye pulled his gaze away from Grace's lithe form gliding through the water. "Oh, yes, thanks, I might take you up on that."

"How are you and Grace getting on?"

Grace? He yanked his attention back to Graham.

"She's a sweet girl with a good heart. Her swim program fits well into your sports theme, doesn't it?" Graham leveled a look at him that made him uneasy.

"Grace's swim program?"

"Who else?"

"Ah, yes." The problem wasn't with her program. Yesterday, she'd made it clear that she believed the problem was his campaign. She didn't want to fit into the rebranded camp; she wanted to scrap the whole plan and start fresh. It didn't seem to matter to her that hours and hours of research supported his decision. The rising enrollment didn't seem to impress her either. "Grace officially presents her program tomorrow afternoon. I expect to offer her a place here." But would she take it?

Who was he kidding? She'd take it and

spend the whole summer bemoaning his plans. He had a knack for saddling himself with women who wanted him to change.

A pang hit his heart. He and Annette would have married this month had he not called off the engagement. He knew it was the right thing to do, but it didn't make it easy. She'd been more in love with the lifestyle his money could provide than with him. He could fix almost any struggling business, but he couldn't fix his relationship with Annette. Ever since then, his mother had pestered him to move back home where she could arrange a neat and tidy marriage to a docile woman of her choice. But he didn't want docile any more than he wanted demanding. He flicked his gaze back to Grace.

If stress caused ulcers, he'd have a stomach full.

Graham tapped his shoulder with the tip of his fishing rod. "Do me a favor and be nice to her."

Kye squirmed at the uncomfortable way Graham studied him. He furrowed his brow. "How exactly do you know each other?"

Graham's sudden laughter relieved the tension between them. "She's my stepdaughter. I thought you knew that."

Stepdaughter? Grace hadn't been waving

at him at all? Heat rushed to his cheeks.

"But your names —"

"She never took my name." Graham's gaze lingered on Grace smoothly pulling her body though the water. "I wished she would, but she was already a teenager when I married her mother."

Kye rubbed his forehead. This crazy woman who prayed over the rescued boy, called him a clown, and stood up to him in his office was related to Ann Douglas? The Ann Douglas who was perfectly groomed and whose dog matched her outfit? It didn't fit. Not even close. Ann seemed like the type who summered at the lake for bragging rights, not because of a nearby camp program. His head spun, and he clambered for a safer topic of conversation. "Uh, has Jeremy chosen his electives yet? They're filling up fast."

Graham's cottage sat on camp property. It fell under a grandfather clause that gave them access to all the camp's programs. They usually took advantage of the kids' club that ran from July 1st to August 31st for their ten-year-old son, Jeremy.

"Thanks for the reminder. I'll get Ann on that. Do you think the new emphasis on sports will be enough to end the season in the black?"

Was Graham really interested in the camp, or was he more interested in the effect closing its doors might have on his property? If the board sold the campground to a private developer, it could potentially raise the value of the existing cottages. Kye suspected a few cottage owners would welcome the news of Camp Moshe closing.

"It'll take more than one season to recoup what was lost the last few years, but if we end this year in the black, there is hope the board will stick it out."

Kye stood shoulder-to-shoulder with Graham, uncomfortable with the sudden silence that swept between them. Grace stood up in the shallows of Moshe Island.

"She's something else, isn't she?" Graham said.

That was one way to describe her. Grace's parting words haunted him afresh. *You won't be able to reinvent the camp in such a short time. Slow down and do something easier. Something more certain.*

Graham slapped his back. "I'm sure you two will figure it out."

Uncertain if that was optimism or instruction, Kye backed away. Graham was a substantial backer to the camp. He couldn't afford to lose his support. He eyed the water warily.

Had Grace told her stepdad what *she* thought of Kye's plans?

Someone who hadn't spent every summer for the last fifteen years swimming in Lake Moshe might find it scary to swim alone, but not Grace. She knew every hidden rock cluster and sand bar like her own home and could, in a heartbeat, navigate toward a safe place to stand if she cramped.

She stood in the shallows of Moshe Island and squinted toward the campground's beach, hardly able to make out her step-dad and Kye talking. She groaned. Were they discussing her? Was Graham telling Kye what she really thought of his program?

She couldn't blame Graham. She'd made it perfectly clear to Kye what she thought of his program yesterday. *What was I thinking running my mouth like that?* She should be buttering up the man, not tearing a strip off of him.

Maybe, if she swam back fast enough, there would be time for damage control. She pushed off. The fresh cold ripped out the last remains of sleepiness, and she automatically moved into her strongest stroke, the front crawl.

She stroked hard, working against the drag. As much as she wanted to smooth things over and secure her place at Camp Moshe, she couldn't swim fast enough to rid herself of Kye and his dangerous plans. His risky ideas stirred frightening memories. Her muscles burned, but she refused to let up.

Job 38 flashed through her mind. Her old habit of reciting Scripture instead of counting strokes kicked in. God laid the foundation of the earth. God determined its measurements. God stretched the line upon it. God is in control. Both during creation and now.

She switched to a butterfly stroke, face down in the water, and never broke rhythm. God laid the cornerstone when the morning stars sang together, and all the sons of God shouted for joy. God. If God was sovereign over everything, then she had to believe He was sovereign over this too. A cramp shot through her side. Kye's plan couldn't be God's will. It just couldn't be.

She let up and rotated on her side to ease the pain. In the distance, a cliff jutted out from the side of the mountain rock. She tried to imagine teens leaping into the lake like Kye had planned. She scanned the beachfront. Images of parasailing, horseback riding, and dirt biking assaulted her mind.

When she'd raised her concerns and tried

to steer Kye toward a safer choice, he'd shut her down. Maybe she should ask Graham if he knew what Kye's problem was. They sure looked buddy-buddy on the beach.

That soured her stomach even more. If her stepdad told Kye about her late-night rant labeling the new camp focus foolish and irresponsible, she was sunk. Kye made it clear he was looking for team players. Yup, she needed to do some serious damage control.

She channeled her anger and increased her speed. She'd find Kye as soon as she got back to shore, and when she did, she'd convince this macho man with a taste for danger that although she believed the camp's future was safer focusing on her project, she could be a team player.

Her fingertips brushed against the stony bottom near the main shore. She stood, and checked the time. One of her best yet. Clearly, swimming angry was good for her pace.

By the time she reached the beach, her mother and Jeremy had ventured out of their cottage and were standing ankle deep in the lake.

"Come on, Mom." Jeremy pouted and then pointed at Grace. "Even Grace is swimming. It's not too cold."

She walked over to them while wringing out her hair. "What's up?"

"Jeremy wants to go in and won't take no for an answer." Ann folded her arms across her chest and looked meaningfully at Grace as if she expected something from her.

"Maybe I can take him in for a short swim." She ruffled his hair.

Her mother frowned. Oh boy, she'd been fishing for a different answer.

"Maybe you can back my decision." Ann gave her a pointed look. "Not every person is as efficient in the water as you."

She faltered. Her mother couldn't be referring to her —

"Good morning."

Grace and Ann spun around at Kye's deep timbre. Did he hear her mother's remark? It wouldn't help her sell her program if he discovered why her own mother doubted her ability to keep Jeremy safe in the water.

"Good morning, Kye." By the time Ann faced Kye, her tone and expression had transformed from sour to sweet. "I was just telling Jeremy that it is unwise to swim in such cold water. What do you think?"

Her mother's words burned Grace's cheeks. Did Kye feel the undercurrent churning between them?

Kye focused on Ann. "I think it's wiser to

ask someone who has been in the water." He shifted those piercing blue eyes to her. "What do you say, Grace? Was it too cold or refreshing?"

Kye took her side? She fought the urge to smile, a response her mother wouldn't find amusing. His steady gaze bolstered Grace's confidence, and the chemistry between them sizzled. She glanced at her mom, who quickly adjusted her shocked expression into one of compromise.

"Ah, I found it refreshing, but I like a cool morning swim. It wakes me up." Kye's unexpected support forced her to reevaluate her original opinion of him. Maybe she'd packed him inside the wrong box yesterday?

"You can take him in up to his waist, no further." Her mother gave Kye a sharp nod and then walked away.

"Yay!" Jeremy thrust his fist in the air. Probably because the water connected to their property measured waist deep or less for meters and meters. They'd been given a pretty long leash. "Come on, Grace, I'll race you!" He took off.

Grace followed Kye's gaze, which followed her mother's retreat to where she settled on the back deck watching them. "Your mom has some strong feelings about the water.

It's like she's afraid of it."

She heard his unasked question, but she wasn't ready to tell him about her mother's aversion to water. Not him. Not anyone.

"I'd better get in there with Jeremy. I promised her I'd take care of him."

He flashed a dimpled smile that further softened her heart. She still didn't like his rebranding ideas, but maybe, just maybe, they could work on the same team toward the common goal of saving the camp. Time would tell.

Her once heavy heart suddenly felt buoyant with possibilities.

# 3

"I'll need to train one assistant in case I'm ever sick, and I've already chosen her. Debbie MacBea is waiting for the official green light, and then she'll come. And that's Water Survival for Non-swimmers in a nutshell." Grace busied herself collecting her notes and putting them back into her folder. She didn't dare look at Kye. Not just yet. If she saw rejection on his face she'd die. Sixty horrendous seconds passed. 61, 62, 63. Finally, when she couldn't take it any longer, she chanced a glance.

He sat there. Fingertips pressed together. Quiet. Watching her.

She straightened, stilled her hands, and watched him right back. His tanned complexion told her how much he enjoyed his morning beach runs. Blonde hair that fell over his eye that first day they met at the beach and again later, when he was running, was now styled into place with a professional polish that probably made the city girls swoon. His tired, blue eyes crinkled at the corners. It was such a shame that exhaustion tainted his lovely eyes. She hoped she wasn't the cause.

He ran a hand through his hair, a movement she had begun to recognize as frustration. A stray piece fell onto his forehead. She suspected the well-formed man wouldn't appreciate it being out of place.

"Are you OK?" It slipped out before she could censor it. Somehow asking such a personal question didn't seem right in an interview.

His eyes widened. At her concern or boldness?

"You look, I don't know. Sort of . . ." Her voice petered off. Where was she going with this?

His soft chuckle came low and swift. "Insulting my looks is not going to sway me to your side."

A blush heated her cheeks. She hurried to cover the awkward moment and stuffed her remaining papers into her bag. "Sorry, I didn't mean —"

"Did you tack that note to my cabin door?" he interrupted. He tilted his head to the side and watched her closely.

She squirmed under his intense scrutiny.

41

"What? No. A note about what?"

He studied her longer, eventually relenting. "It's nothing. Forget it."

She clutched the straps of her bag that held her presentation material. Years of hard work. "We're off track. Do you see why my program is right for the camp?"

"It's good. Very good," he conceded.

"And more than enough to save it from closure," she pushed.

Nothing.

She felt a big "but" coming —

"But it's not enough to sway the entire direction of the summer," he said.

Her heart hit her toes. "Why? Water programs are a no-brainer for camps. Add water skiing, tubing, a little wake boarding and paddle boarding, and this place will be swimming with kids."

He smiled again, and the dimple that flashed in his cheek weakened her knees. She averted her gaze to the bookcase behind Kye. He had lined his shelves with the same authors she enjoyed.

"Those are all good ideas and planned activities, but according to my research, three of our competing camps already offer those activities. Camp Moshe needs to stand out. Be unique."

Nope, just because they read the same

novels didn't mean they were on the same page. He was just like every other guy she knew, totally unwilling to admit he was wrong. She folded her arms across her chest. "Extreme sports are dangerous."

He raised an unconcerned eyebrow. "Then strap on your helmet. It might get bumpy."

"Strap on my helmet?" she echoed. "All we need is one kid to overestimate his ability, one kid who doesn't listen and gets hurt, and all the signed waivers in the world won't protect this place from closure."

He simultaneously rubbed his thumb and index finger across both eyebrows.

If she hadn't caused his exhaustion, she definitely caused his irritation. It pricked her conscience.

"Life is dangerous, Grace. You can't live in a padded box."

Her eyes dampened. No one knew better than her how dangerous and unfair the world could be.

"Look," he shifted in his seat. "You don't have to like the idea, but you do need to back it. I expect all my staff to fully support my decisions in public."

"So I can disagree as long as I don't tell anyone? How convenient for you." She tucked her presentation bag under her arm, ready to storm out.

Disappointment flashed across his face, coming and going so fast she wondered if she imagined it. She dismissed the silly notion. Why would he care if she stayed or not?

He flipped closed the file folder that held her name. "You can tell as many people as you like, but you won't do it on my payroll."

"But —"

He cut her off with a downward swipe of his hand. "Look, I've given you a large chunk of my day. You are welcome to stay. I think your program fits well into our plans. But if you can't get on board with the re-branded camp, then you should consider taking your program elsewhere."

"What?"

"Let me know your decision by the end of the day."

She stood there. Numb.

He continued as if he hadn't just pulled the rug out from under her world. "We have a cabin set aside for the Director of Water Activities, but if you prefer to stay with your family we can free it up as a rental. There are less than four weeks left until the campers arrive. So it's get on board or get out. Your choice."

She stomped through the wooded trail slapping twigs and leaves out of her way. The path she beat down led from the office back to the privately owned cottages.

*Get on board or get out. Who does he think he is?* If he thought he could bully her to his side, he had another think coming. If she didn't run her pilot program now, she'd have to wait another year to apply at other camps, and by then she'd be too old for the young entrepreneurs grant. No one else would add such a big program so late in the season. She had been counting on Uncle Carl. Tears stung her eyes, but she refused to let them fall. Getting out was not an option. She'd invested far too much.

She slumped against a tree and swatted a mosquito. If his crazy sports idea failed, Camp Moshe would close. She couldn't lose Camp Moshe, but she couldn't back a program that she believed was dangerous either.

*What should I do?*

This had been the last place her whole family was happy. Her best memories were here. Losing it would be like losing Dad and Becky all over again. She pushed off the tree — this time much slower — scooping to pick up a trail of garbage left by a previous hiker. She sent a simple prayer heavenward and plodded the rest of the way to their family cottage. *Please Lord. Please save this place. Save my memories. Show me what to do.*

"Grace, is that you?" Her mother called from the back deck the minute her feet hit the wood.

Great. Last night and this morning she'd managed to avoid her mother and the inevitable showdown. She tossed the garbage into their bear-proof bin and dragged herself around back where she found her mom sitting in a lounge chair, stirring a straw in a glass filled with ice cubes. "Yes?"

"Jeremy, can you please refill my iced tea?"

"Sure mom." Jeremy scampered off, shooting Grace a sympathetic look. The hammer was set to drop.

Mom repositioned herself in her chair. "I would like to discuss what happened yesterday morning on the beach."

She leaned against the deck railing, raised her eyebrows, and pretended she didn't know what her mother referred to. "What happened?"

"You humiliated me in front of the camp staff."

"What?"

"Don't think I didn't see the looks that passed between you and that camp director."

"Interim director," she corrected.

"I will not be made a fool of."

"Mom, that's not what —"

"Enough, Grace. As long as you live under my roof, you will support my decisions. Understood?"

Support her decisions. Support Kye's decisions. When would she be allowed to support her own decisions? When would her opinion count? But Mom was right about one thing. Enough was enough.

"Fine, Mom. You've made a hard decision very easy. I'll be moving into a camp cabin as soon as I officially accept the position as the Director of Water Activities."

Silence.

She couldn't stem the flow of disappointment that her mother's indifference caused. What did she expect anyway? She spun around and strode back into the woods toward the camp offices. She'd tell Kye right away and get to work cleaning her cabin.

Kye. Straight from the frying pan into the fire.

She pushed back the tree limbs and leaves encroaching on the trail and swiped a few tears as she went. *Why aren't you listening, God?*

Wisdom from long ago rushed back so clear and intense she could almost hear her father's husky voice.

"Just because God is silent doesn't mean He isn't listening."

OK, so maybe He was listening, but she sure didn't like that He was leading her to sizzle in Kye's frying pan of dangerous ideas.

She pushed open the camp office door and breezed past Judy, faking a confidence she didn't quite feel.

Judy leapt to her feet. "Mr. Campton is on a ca—"

"I'll let myself in." Adrenaline thrust her forward, and she entered Kye's office a half step before Judy.

"I'm sorry, Mr. Campton," Judy apologized as Kye's eyes widened at the intrusion. "She insisted —"

"I bullied my way in," Grace said. No need for Judy to take a hit for her rudeness. Grace blinked back tears, willing the heat rising on her face to recede.

Kye disconnected his call. "Thank you, Judy." He waited until Judy left and closed the door behind her. Then he looked directly at Grace.

She squirmed and shifted her weight from one foot to the other. She should have thought this through a bit better. She lifted her chin. "I'll take the job, and I'll need the cabin."

If Kye was surprised, he hid it well. "What

changed your mind?" His voice hitched in an odd way. Was he worried their earlier interaction was the cause of her grief?

For a brief second, she considered letting him think his bullying attitude caused her pain, but her conscience pricked. "My mother," she admitted. "It's time I made my own decisions, and it became clear tonight that I can't do that from home." One tear came dangerously close to escaping. She faked brushing back her hair to swipe it before it could fall.

Kye pushed back his chair and stood. He reached a hand across the desk, and the tiniest smile turned up the corners of his lips. "Welcome to Camp Moshe. It's what your Uncle Carl wanted."

She let him enfold her palm in his, and heat radiated up her arm, warming her cheeks again. She forced another smile. What had she gotten herself into?

How did he get here?

Kye looked across the restaurant table at his mother and Grace chatting like old friends. After only a few minutes of pleasantries, they began clucking away and it had lasted the entire meal.

"He always was a difficult boy." His mother nodded in agreement to something

Grace whispered under her breath.

Great. They'd joined forces. That made things awkward, to say the least. Although he seemed to be the only uncomfortable one at the moment. His mother was glowing, and Grace looked the most relaxed he'd ever seen her. Although to be fair, he'd only seen her swimming or in his office fighting for her program. Unless she was the hooded figure fleeing his cabin after slipping a second threat under his door. He narrowed his eyes. Could it have been Grace?

"Just water, thanks," he said to the waiter hovering over his mug with a pot of coffee. "Could we get the b—"

A crash from the kitchen burst through the dining room. "Excuse me a moment, sir." The waiter scurried away.

Great. He needed to wrap this up before Mom pulled out the baby pictures she still kept in her wallet.

His mother laughed at something else Grace said and it landed with a jab to the heart. He'd have to burst her bubble at some point. This wasn't a date. But would it hurt to let Mom believe it was? He hated the thought of dousing the hope in her eyes. And, as a bonus, it had paused their ongoing dialogue about why he hadn't given her grandkids yet.

"Did Kye ever tell you about the time he rode his bike off the garage roof? He was certain that kind of training was needed if he wanted to be a professional BMX racer." His mom leaned across the table a little closer to Grace, totally in her element.

OK. This had to end. And the sooner the better. Thankfully, the waiter was approaching the table again. He lifted his hand to motion for the bill when Grace caught the waiter's eye and motioned to her teacup. The waiter lifted the pot in his hand and hurried over.

"Thank you." Grace smiled as he poured her tea. She stirred a teaspoon of honey into the hot beverage. "Tell me everything," she whispered conspiratorially to his mother, tossing him a teasing smile. "The more dirt I have on him, the better." Her spoon clinked against the china cup and saucer like a falling judge's gavel sentencing him to coffee and dessert.

His half-raised hand fell onto his lap. Grace's eyes danced as his mom embellished the story of that "fateful summer he nearly killed himself." Even he had to smile. Maybe it was worth it. So what if Mom thought this was a date?

When Grace had burst back through his office doors and accepted the camp position with all his conditions, his vow to keep a professional distance between himself and employees flew out the window. It had taken every ounce of control he could muster to resist swiping his thumb across her moist cheek. For one heart-crunching second, he thought his my-way-or-the-highway stance had caused her tears.

"Human catapult?" Grace arched a brow and gave him a questioning look.

Great. Mom had moved onto that story. He shrugged and grinned, happy to provide comic relief on what appeared to have been a very bad day.

Before Grace left, she had told him about her fight with her mom. He thought he had mother issues! The worst he'd dealt with was surprise matchmaking. Grace's mom was a whole other bag of tricks. Now *she* seemed like the type to slip in a threat or two to manipulate things into going her way.

"He didn't?" Grace gasped. As his mother egged on Grace, Grace's laughter filled the intimate dining space. Everything about her sparkled.

"Excuse me, sir. This was left for you at the bar." A waiter slipped a folded notecard to Kye. The women kept chattering.

"Thank you." He accepted the note. All he'd meant to do was offer Grace a listening ear. Some kindness. But before he knew it, he'd leapt over the professional lines behind which he'd lived his entire career and invited her to dinner. It was like his subconscious had seized control, and he couldn't stop the words from leaving his mouth. Grace clearly needed a night away from her family, and he needed a buffer between him and his mom. Win-win. Right?

But did she think they were on a real date?

Her simple sundress and loose hair looked casual enough, but what did he know about how women dress for dates? He hadn't been on one since his failed engagement.

Unless he counted his mother's poor victims.

Well, however they labeled tonight, he owed Grace a thank you. Her laughter had loosened the perpetually tight muscles in his neck. He rubbed the side of his neck. Nah, that was silly. He'd just finally relaxed. It had nothing to do with Grace.

Yet here they were.

With his mother.

On a date.

He hid a smile and opened the note. *You were warned.*

Kye jumped up and his chair knocked a waiter, who, with impressive agility, spun and bowed to present a silver tray of several dessert options to their table. "Can I interest anyone in dessert?"

"Ah, ladies?" Kye wrung one hand around his neck and slunk back to his seat. The surrounding tables were filled with couples or small families, and the bar was empty. No one seemed out of place. Whoever wrote the note was long gone.

"Oh, I couldn't eat another bite. That was the best meal I've had in ages, but thank you," Grace answered. She curiously watched him. Could she have masterminded things so the note would be delivered in her presence and throw him off?

The waiter turned slightly toward his mother. "No, thank you. Not tonight." She touched Grace's forearm, which rested on the table. "Let me tell you another story."

Grace's animated response to his mother seemed as innocent as an animated princess. But Annette had taught him that looks could be deceiving.

Grace dabbed the corners of her eyes with her napkin as his mom relived another chapter from his youth. "That must have been terrible. But it's so funny to hear you tell it now!"

"It was terrible. Some mothers had the terrible twos. I had the terrible teens. There were days I thought I was losing my mind."

"Well, I'm all grown up now, Mom," Kye cut in. "No more homemade garage ramps or catapults."

"But still as senseless as ever. I mean, gracious. If I hadn't kept such a close eye on you," she placed her hand over Kye's and gave her best stern look, "you'd be six feet under."

"You exaggerate, Mom." He tugged his hand back.

"He must have some sense. His business track record speaks volumes. You're a good man, Malachi Campton," Grace gently interjected.

Her unexpected praise caused him to straighten in his seat. Did she mean he was good at his job? A good person? Why did it matter to him that she thought he was good?

Oblivious to the undercurrent churning between Kye and Grace, his mom asked, "So Grace, what do you think of my Malachi's Extreme Sports Camp?"

No, this was not good. Not good at all. Time to shut it down. "Mom —"

"No, it's OK," Grace assured him.

What was she doing?

"I think it's risky," she continued, "and it definitely moves me out of my comfort zone. But I'm beginning to see that sometimes God wants us to be uncomfortable, so when He does great things, we know it was all Him and none of us."

Huh? He hadn't seen that coming.

His mother's mouth briefly slackened into a perfect O before she snapped it closed. Clearly she thought she'd found an advocate for her own agenda. The corner of his lip twitched. Grace wasn't shaping up to be who either of them expected.

"You think the camp deal is risky," Tamera recovered quickly, but her tone lost the edge of humor it had carried earlier in the evening. "Let me tell you about Malachi's risk history. I wouldn't let Malachi ride a dirt bike, so what does he do? He goes to his buddy's house and rides his. Blows through a stop sign and gets clipped by a van."

"Mom, it wasn't that big of a deal —"

"Not that big of a deal? Five stitches are a big deal." She took his chin in her hands and tilted his head. "See this," she said to Grace, "That's where the scar on his chin came from. Now the scar on his shoulder, that happened —"

"OK, OK," Kye pulled out of his mother's hands. "I think that's enough storytelling for tonight. What will we talk about next time if you tell her all my secrets now?"

Next time? Why on earth did he say that?

Employers do not date their employees.

His mother pounced. "Speaking of next time, why don't you both come for Sunday dinner? Your chapel ends at noon, right? I can have it ready for one o'clock."

"Mom I —"

"We'd love to, Tamera. Thank you," Grace cut in.

*What?*

Grace's guileless expression offered no clue as to her motive.

Was she like Annette, a master of passive-aggressive manipulation? Or worse, willing to resort to violence to get her way?

He forced a smile. If Grace was behind these threats, he owed his mother a thank you for the invite. How did that saying go? Keep your friends close and your enemies closer.

# 4

Kye had been avoiding her for two days, and for the life of her, Grace couldn't figure out what she had done to upset him. He lifted the barbeque lid and slapped some patties onto the sizzling grill outside the camp kitchen. He only stood about four feet from her, but it might as well have been a mile.

She'd grabbed a bag of hamburger buns and carted it to the buffet table — picnic tables strung together in a line. It didn't make sense. She'd done nothing but toe the line since moving onto the campgrounds and into the cabin next to his. She had been tempted to voice her opinions when the staff first arrived and began discussing the summer schedule, but she had kept her word to publically support Kye. She wandered back toward the kitchen.

Kye flipped the patties on the grill, and a cloud of smoke drifted into the sky. He talked shop with twin brothers Eric and Kaleb, expert rock climbers.

"The kids will love it," enthused Eric.

"How long will it take you to set up the ropes and stuff?" Kye flipped another burger.

Grace touched the exterior wall of the kitchen to steady herself. The idea of kids scaling walls of rock left her dizzy.

None of the guys took any notice. "Should I use my power of invisibility to fight crime or for evil?" she mused.

"What was that?" Kaleb glanced her way.

"Oh, nothing," she mumbled, fighting the urge to laugh.

Eric and Kaleb slipped right back into a story of their latest climb, and Kye focused so intently on the grill that she half expected it to burst into flames or do some other act of marvelous wonder.

This had to be about their dinner date. She placed her hand on her stomach to ease a rush of queasiness that had nothing to do with endangered campers or fighting crime.

Why didn't she turn him down? She wasn't interested in dating. She had assumed he'd invited her to a business dinner to hammer out the details of her new role.

She propped open the kitchen door with a thick branch broken off of a nearby tree, slipped inside, and grabbed the potato chips. She tried to catch Kye's eye as she passed on her return to the picnic tables.

Nothing.

She had stewed the entire ride to the restaurant over ways to gently let him down in case their business dinner turned romantic, while mentally arguing that it wasn't a date. It couldn't be a date. Then, he'd introduced her to his mother. *His mother!*

She dropped the chips onto the picnic table beside the container holding mustard, relish, and ketchup. He was the one that crossed the line from professional to personal, so why was he freezing her out?

He leaned in toward the boys, giving them his full attention. His casual shorts and graphic T-shirt made him look like one of the guys rather than the man in charge. He adapted to his environment like a chameleon. Previously, he pulled off the polished office look perfectly. But this look — casual, confident in his skin, not trying to impress anyone — was the look she liked best. Should she pull him from Eric and Kaleb and just tell him that she wasn't interested in romance? That she wasn't the type to date her boss? Or anyone for that matter.

She had spent most of their meal together alternating between making nice with his mom and trying to figure out how in the world she was going to dump her boss.

He laughed at something they said.

She wasn't interested in dating him. But if that was really the case, why was she obsessing over him?

"You OK?" Kate, her longtime friend, touched her arm. Kate also happened to be in charge of the arts and crafts department. At least someone here was on her team.

She tore her eyes from Kye, horrified to realize how much she had actually enjoyed dinner with him. *Ugh!* A lot of good that did her. Clearly, he didn't enjoy dinner with her. Why else would he avoid her like the plague?

"I'm fine, thanks."

Kate followed her gaze to the director. "He's pretty cute," she said in a questioning tone.

"I'm not interested." She wasn't sure who she was trying to convince. Kate? Kye? Or herself?

Kye carried a plate of hot patties to the picnic table and set them down. He cupped his mouth and called out to the fifteen or so college-aged kids splashing in the waves. His eyes skipped over hers. "Dinner's ready!"

Yup, he was avoiding her.

The small group pressed in around her, shuffling her a touch closer to Kye, and he asked the Lord's blessing over the meal. Kate's knowing smile rubbed her raw. Newly engaged, Kate saw romance everywhere.

"Enrollment is up," Kye said. "We have a great summer forecasted, and I can't wait to get all the equipment unloaded and put together."

A cheer went up.

"Today is about getting to know one another and having some fun before the work begins."

"When does the equipment arrive?"

"Sometime this week. I'll assign you all prep work as the stuff arrives. Until then, grab a burger, and have fun. But be careful to clean up after yourself. We don't want to attract raccoons."

Half the crowd hit the table, forcing both Grace and Kye to the outskirts, and the other half started up a game of Ultimate Frisbee. But not even the happy background noise of summer fun could smooth the awkwardness between them.

"Did you need something?" Kye busied himself flicking imaginary sand off his clothing.

"I think *we* need something."

He stilled.

"We need to talk. About dinner —"

"No," he interrupted, "let me go first."

"You've had two days to go first." She didn't say it rudely, but she knew she made her point when soft pink flushed his cheeks.

"I wasn't sure how to tell you. I didn't want to hurt you."

"Tell me what?"

"That dinner wasn't a romantic thing," he said in a whoosh of breath.

She laughed. She didn't mean to, but relief hit like a tidal wave and she couldn't hold it back. His perplexed expression only made her laugh more.

"I know I'm not a super catch or anything, but you don't need to mock me." His dry humor just about did her in.

"No," she put pressure on the sudden cramp in her side caused by her giggle fit. "I've been stressing out about how to let you down easy for days. I thought it was a work dinner, and then your mother shows up. I mean, come on. *Your mother?*"

He cracked a smile. "Yeah, that wasn't cool. The whole thing sort of got out of hand. What was the deal with you accepting Sunday's invite?"

She quieted. "Yeah, sorry about that. I —"

She hesitated. She couldn't tell him that she had begun to enjoy the evening so much that she accepted without thinking it through. "Should we cancel?"

He thought for a minute. "Would you mind keeping it? My mom's pretty intent on seeing me settled into a relationship. If she thinks we've got something cooking, it would give me some breathing space."

If he wasn't worried about a meddling mother and fending off arranged dates, he'd be more focused on saving the camp. It wasn't like they had to lie or anything. They just wouldn't correct her assumption that they were a couple. "Sure. I mean, what harm can it do?"

His cheek dimpled and he leaned in as if he was about to share a secret.

Her new assistant, Debbie, grabbed for a Frisbee but missed it. The disc hit the sand between Grace and Kye, and they jumped apart. The moment was lost.

"Sorry Boss-man," Debbie called from where she lay prone in the sand, having missed the catch. Kye scooped up the plastic disc and faked a throw toward Grace.

She didn't even blink. "You think you can take me?" she taunted.

His eyes twinkled. "Any day, any time." He held it out of her reach with just enough cockiness to send adrenaline surging through her.

She made a sudden grab and snagged the disc. A quick flick of her wrist sent it sailing toward the lake.

"Hey!" He tried to grab her arm but missed.

She shrieked, running toward the water. "Beat you!" She ripped off her bathing suit cover-up as she ran and tossed it on the sand. He took off after her.

When the water hit her waist, she lost her footing and splashed down. Kye caught her arm and pulled her up. She spluttered and coughed. His laugh crinkled the corners of his boyish eyes. He should laugh more. It made the blue flecks in them sparkle.

Water streamed down her cheeks, and she shook her head. An unreadable look crossed Kye's face, and he dropped her arm. He looked at her with . . . interest?

She snagged the floating Frisbee and used it to send a surge of water his way, and she let the waves tug them apart. Uncertainty washed over her heart. She couldn't let a summer attraction affect her plans. She'd worked too hard to lose focus now. "I have to . . . to . . . I have to go."

She trotted out of the surf and shrugged into her cover-up. She needed to get away.

Away from Kye. Away from any distraction that might move her focus from her goal.

"Wait!"

She ignored him, grabbed a few bags of chips and snacks as a makeshift dinner, and headed for her cabin.

He caught her arm, swung her around, and the chips went flying. "What happened back there?"

She couldn't explain it. She needed to focus on her program, not some summer romance with a man who made it abundantly clear he wasn't available. She owed that to her dad. To Becky.

"I feel like I did something wrong." His voice softened.

Kate watched them from the kitchen door with an *I-knew-it* smile on her face.

"Grace?"

She hardened herself against the catch in his voice and stepped back, putting a respectable amount of space between them. "It's nothing. It's me. I just remembered something that I needed to do. Don't worry about it."

"If you're certain —"

"I am."

"OK." He turned and headed back to the group.

She slumped against a tree, hating how

things had unquestionably shifted between them.

From the perch on his cabin porch Kye had a direct line of sight to Grace sitting on her cabin steps, morning coffee in hand, Bible open, eyes closed. He really should get to work. Get a start on his day. But something drew him to her. Something undeniable. Against his better judgment, he headed her way.

He hit the bottom step and saw the note. He ripped it down as exasperation shot through his veins. *This is your last chance to leave.*

A twig snapped in the woods. He spun around and peered into the trees. Nothing. He stilled and listened.

Quiet. Unnaturally quiet.

These notes were probably harmless. He'd received threats of various kinds at other jobs. But for some reason, this time they had him all worked up. His gaze dropped to the ground as he focused his hearing and noticed some markings. A closer look and his chest seized like a vise grip. Bear tracks leading toward Grace's cabin.

The note slipped from his fingers. He whipped around at a new rustling. Nothing. He twisted back to Grace, still meditating on God's Word, completely unaware and exposed.

He jogged over to her. "Good morning."

"Morning, Mr. Fix-it." She didn't add the *good.* Was that on purpose? Despite yesterday's obvious, almost insulting relief that she wasn't interested in him romantically, something had definitely shifted between them. Whether that shift was good or bad remained to be seen.

"We have a potential problem."

She arched a brow but said nothing.

"There are some bear tracks leading up to your place . . ." He wasn't ready to share details of the threatening notes.

"What?" She leapt to her feet and scanned the trees behind him.

"I'm fairly certain he's gone, but I'll walk you to camp."

She hesitated long enough that he stumbled to add, "It's on my way to the office."

She nodded. "Let me grab my things."

They walked in silence, both listening carefully for any sounds out of the ordinary. She stood in her flip-flops and beach attire and he in his leather oxfords and business clothes. It was hard to believe they worked at the same place.

Her rigid gait lacked her usual poise, and a tiny vein pulsed in a rhythmic beat in her neck. She jacked her shoulders up to her earlobes. To say she was frightened was an understatement. He almost reached out and placed a comforting hand at the small of her back but caught himself in time. He stuffed his hand into his pocket. "So, ah, what were you studying back there?"

"I'm working through Proverbs." Her voice wobbled a bit.

Her refreshing faith was beautiful — probably the most beautiful thing about her — and that said a lot because she was a striking woman. Her genuine love for the Lord shone through during their staff prayer times. Grace had proven to be very different from Annette. "Any special reason you chose Proverbs?"

She searched the trees, still on high alert. "Just looking for wisdom."

He got it. She didn't want to talk about it. Why should she? She hardly knew him. "Then Proverbs is a good place to start."

Silence descended again, only broken by a rustling in the leaves behind them. "Did you hear that?"

She froze. "What?"

"That!" He pointed to a black bear crouching in the bushes and staring at them. He shoved Grace behind him and racked his brain. Should he look him in the eye?

Should he shout? He looked over the bear's shoulder and roared, "Get out of here. Go!" He slowly backed up, nudging Grace toward the camp.

He could hear her fervent prayers pressed into his back.

The bear stood to its full height, and for a terrifying moment Kye was sure the bear sized him up. But for whatever reason, the bear dropped back down and lumbered away into the thicker woods. Kye didn't even know he'd been holding his breath until it rocketed out of his body.

Grace pressed deeper against him and released her grip on the waist of his shirt. "Thank you, God," she whispered.

"Amen," he echoed.

He spun and gave Grace a not-so-gentle shove. "Let's get out of here!"

They took off as though the woods were on fire, and he steered her toward the safety of the dining hall. The cook always arrived early so the doors were bound to be open. Panting, he flung open the door so hard it bounced on its hinges. He held it as Grace slipped inside. His heart lurched at her trembling. He shut the door and scanned the wooded area surrounding the dining hall.

"Oh!" Her quiet gasp ripped his gaze from

the trees.

The dining hall was trashed.

"Bobby? Bobby?" He strode through the mess toward the swinging doors leading into the prep area while calling out for their cook. This was Bobby's first year with Camp Moshe, and this was hardly the best way to start.

Bobby came through the doors shaking his head. "Mr. Campton, I was just about to call you."

"What happened?" He couldn't believe his eyes. Two broken windows left shattered glass all over the floor, and there were clear claw marks on the window frames. A few overturned tables were rammed against each other, and there were long scuff marks on the floor.

"Best I can tell is that a bear got into the kitchen."

"How?"

"The back door didn't click shut. There was a wedge of a branch stuck inside. Just enough for the bear to push it open."

"But the glass?"

Bobby shrugged.

Kye turned toward Grace. "Have there ever been bears here before?"

She shrugged.

"I heard from some of the returning staff

that black bears have been spotted, but not too often. I have a shotgun locked in the back cabinet in the kitchen," Bobby said.

"A shotgun?" Grace's voice squeaked.

Man, this was getting worse by the second.

Bobby flicked a glance her way. "The cabinet's locked. Besides, it's a special one. Designed to shoot blanks. It's called a bear banger. The noise scares them away."

"That can't be safe," Grace challenged.

"Safer than this."

Grace huffed.

Point taken.

"We had them at a camp out west. My experience is that once a bear hits the mother lode like this," Bobby continued, "they can be pretty aggressive. He's likely coming back."

"Coming back?" Grace's shrill voice cut through him. "We have campers arriving in a few weeks. Coming back is not an option."

Kye moved in front of Grace and stooped down so they were eye-to-eye. He placed both hands on her upper arms and gave her a gentle squeeze. "It'll be OK. I'll fix this." He turned back to Bobby. "Any idea of what drew him here?"

"Hasn't been a good spring for berries and such. When the pickings get slim, they tend to wander in looking for food. There were some chips and snack items strewn around the woods back there." He pointed towards Grace's cabin. "That's likely what first caught his attention."

"I'm so sorry," Grace cut in. "This is all my fault. You warned us about not leaving food around, and then when my chips . . ." Her voice trailed off, and his heart ached for her torment.

"What happened here?" As the staff wandered in for breakfast, their jaws hit the floor. Bobby filled them in.

"Dude, how are we going to fix that before the campers arrive?" Eric stared at the ceiling.

Kye looked up. How on earth did the bear pull down ceiling tiles?

He dropped his eyes back to Grace, who stood hunched over like the weight on her shoulders was too heavy to carry.

"Grace?" He spoke soft enough that the noise from the staff covered his words. "I spun you around. I was the one who dropped the snacks. This is not your fault." He could tell by the look in her eyes that she wasn't buying it.

"So what do we do?" Grace asked.

I don't know about you," Bobby interrupted, "but I'll take inventory and head into town for more supplies. I got a boatload of hungry kids descending soon and this animal emptied my cupboards. You," he directed his gaze at Kye. "You gotta find a way to stop that thing from coming back or consider postponing the start of camp."

Kye nodded, suddenly grateful that he took a chance and hired Bobby. He'd been leery about hiring someone from across the country after a phone interview, but despite Bobby's young age of twenty-two, he came with great references, previous experience as a camp cook, and a surprising knowledge of bears.

Kye snagged a notepad and pencil from the counter and walked out of the dining hall and felt Grace hot on his heels. "What are you going to do?" she asked.

"I'm going to see what kind of damage he caused and pray he doesn't come back."

He rounded the back to where the door had been propped open for yesterday's barbeque. He jotted down details as he spoke. "Looks like our friend pulled away a few boards here." He pointed to the exterior by the door jamb. "Ripped it right to the plywood here." He pointed again and made some more notes.

"And it looks like some of the plywood has been chipped off too." Grace leaned in for a closer look.

Her light vanilla scent caught him off-guard.

"Are these teeth marks?"

He held his breath unwilling to taste her again. Talk about needing the wisdom of Proverbs. "Looks like it." He clenched his teeth until his jaw ached.

"Maybe you should call someone?" she suggested, oblivious to his discomfort.

"Good idea." He pulled out his phone and searched up the number for the Ministry of Natural Resources. After a short wait, he was connected to the proper people. She folded her arms across her middle and rocked on her heels, listening to his side of the conversation as he filled them in. She tapped her foot.

"What do you mean by aggressive?" Kye said.

Grace stepped closer. "Aggressive?" she echoed.

"Do you really think that's necessary?"

"What's necessary?" she whispered. She clearly wanted him to pull the phone back so she could hear.

He turned away from her. "I will. Thank you." He disconnected.

"What did they say?"

"It's not sounding too good. He said bears are pretty smart and curious, and that if he finds food, he'll keep coming back. He might become aggressive."

"Aggressive? How long will he keep coming back?"

"Sometimes weeks, months, or even years."

"We don't have that long!"

"Because of the nature of this problem, and the fact we saw the bear this morning, they are going to look into removing him."

"Kill him?" Her eyes widened.

"No, relocate him." He smiled at her obvious relief. "I'll call them back in a bit, and they'll tell me the game plan."

"This is not what Camp Moshe needs right now."

"Yeah, you can say that again." It wasn't what he needed either.

# 5

---

"Tell the reporters I'm busy." He slammed the phone down and prayed Judy would prove to be a great administrative assistant and handle the gathering vultures circling for a story. Could the day get any worse?

"Bad time?" Grace poked her head into his office.

"Bad morning," he grumbled. The snap of a camera flash made him jump from his desk and usher her into the room. He closed the door behind her, shutting out the media.

She clomped across his office in the heaviest steel-toed boots he'd ever seen on a woman and carried an odd-looking canister on her hip. She fell onto the stuffed chair that sat across from his desk, rested one boot-clad ankle over the opposite knee, and settled back into a comfortable position that implied she was staying awhile.

"What on earth are you wearing?" He crossed the room and leaned against the front of his desk.

"Protection." She didn't miss a beat. "And this," she proudly lifted her canister and shook it, "is homemade pepper spray."

Great. And some cameraman just got it all on film.

"And that?" He pointed at the rusty chain hanging off her belt with odds and ends strung through it.

"A noise maker. If I'm walking through the trails, I want the bear to hear me and run away."

Clearly, she'd done some internet research. "And that?"

She casually unsheathed a hunting knife stuffed into a holder inside her boot. "It's Graham's knife, and no, I'm not crazy so wipe that look off your face. I will not be caught unprepared again." She slid the knife back into its holder and shifted her position.

He fought to keep a straight face. Somehow he knew if he cracked even the faintest smile he might be on the receiving end of whatever homemade concoction was bubbling in that canister. "I highly doubt that little knife is going to do much against a black bear."

"Well I don't have a gun license . . ."

He folded his arms across his chest.

Enough was enough. The last thing he needed was a posse of vigilantes saddling up to save the day. He was the boss. He would do the saving.

"Look, we need to —" the shrill of the phone cut him off.

He twisted around and snapped it up, "Yes?" and then softened. "Hi, Mom. I'm fine. I thought you were another reporter digging around."

"Say hi for me," Grace whispered. He waved her off.

"Yes, that's Grace." He scowled at her, and she crossed her eyes and stuck out her tongue.

He couldn't help but smile. "Mom says hi to you as well." He covered the phone's mouthpiece with his hand and whispered, "She's happy you're here with me."

She patted her hair and struck a ridiculous model pose in her crazy anti-bear get-up. "Of course she is."

He focused on his mother. "We have to bail on lunch . . . I know . . . Yes . . . then you're the only one that doesn't know."

Grace leaned forward intently as he summarized what happened this morning. It felt good not to face his determined mother alone for a change.

"It's all over the news, Mom. A bear . . .

yes, I know they can be dangerous . . . OK. I will. I love you too, Mom."

"So, lunch is off?" She sat back into the chair.

"Yeah, but honestly, I would have rather faced my mom and a room full of relatives expecting to meet my future bride than deal with this bear disaster."

Her eyes widened at the word *bride.*

"I didn't mean *bride.* I mean, well, my mom would have made a big deal out of you and . . ."

Her soft laughter stopped his babbling and he shook his head. When was he going to learn to filter his words? The unintentional thoughts and invitations that slipped from his lips infuriated him.

"Don't worry. I haven't gone and registered for towels or anything. Besides," she quipped, arching a perfectly shaped brow. "I have no intention of getting my foot caught in a marriage trap. It's not husband season. It's bear season."

The tension in his shoulders eased a bit more. Odd, how she was the only one who seemed to be able to loosen that perpetual knot in his neck.

"So what can I do to help?" she asked.

"Do you hunt?" he teased.

"Only during wabbit season." She nailed

Elmer Fudd.

He clicked on the TV and pressed play on the recording he made of an earlier newscast. "Did you see this?"

A reporter zoomed in on a picture of a black bear lumbering into the woods, flipped to a shot of a bear trap, then relayed comments made by a staff member wishing to remain anonymous.

"Who spoke to the news?" Her genuine surprise assured him that she wasn't the one to leak the story.

He shrugged. "I don't know. But it was just enough for a few anxious parents to pull their kids from our first week."

"I'm sorry." She really did look sorry.

"Hey, they quote you." She pointed back at the screen as the picture zoomed in on the outside of the office, and his quote played over the still picture. "Why did you speak to them?"

"They phoned and were running with the story either way. The truth is better than what people might imagine. We spotted a black bear, and we suspect it's the same one that damaged the dining hall, and we are taking the necessary steps to relocate it before the campers arrive. End of story."

She didn't look impressed. "If that's the end of the story, why the scrunchy, angry

face and shoulders hitched to your earlobes?"

He forced his shoulders to relax. "Because
that's not the spin the news is putting on it.
The way they are talking, we are under attack. I'm shocked all the parents haven't
yanked their kids after this irresponsible
report ran."

"Neither of us can afford to lose campers.
Your job and my program depend on a suc-
cessful summer. Let's put our heads together and get rid of this bear."

"Maybe we should add hunting as an
extreme sport option and make taking down
the bear the ultimate prize?" He was joking,
of course, but he backpedaled when her face
paled. "You know I'm kidding, right?"

"Yeah, I know. It just reminded me of how
big he was when he stood up. I thought he
was going to charge."

"Honestly, so did I." He didn't want to
think about what might have happened had
the bear charged.

"It was pretty sweet the way you shoved
me behind you." The corners of her lips
turned up.

"Couldn't have that vanilla scent you wear
drawing him closer, could we?"

She blushed.

Why on earth did he say that?

"So, what's next? Are we heading out to set traps? I cleared my schedule so I can help."

Help was the last thing he expected from her. The way she quivered at any mention of danger, he expected her to hole up in her cabin armed with bear spray and a rifle until this was settled.

"There's no need —"

"This camp is just as important to me as it is to you." She set her jaw in a determined look. "What are you doing to protect the staff?"

"All the staff are carrying bear spray, *real* bear spray. And they're walking in pairs." He sent a wry look her way. "Except you, of course. You've taken care of yourself. I also instructed them to stay off the trails."

"The same trails you need the kids to ride their mountain bikes down in a few short weeks?"

This was a nightmare.

"Kye, you have a call on line one." Judy buzzed in.

He sighed and picked up the phone. "Yes, yes, we are doing everything we can to assure the safety of the children . . . The trap is on its way here now . . . Yes. A conservation officer will relocate it. No, we are not interested in selling at this point."

Sell? Grace's large eyes widened.

"I have your number if that changes." He disconnected.

"Sell? The board is considering selling Camp Moshe?"

"Not really. A local developer is pushing hard for a sale. He's actually Eric and Kaleb's dad."

"The rock-climbing twins?"

"Yup. Most of the lakefront property here is taken. Camp land is the only land left with beach access. The offers have been coming in steady since the word got out we were in financial trouble. This guy hoped to capitalize on the bear scare."

"Do you think they told their dad and then leaked the story to tip the scales their way?"

Hmm. He hadn't thought of that.

She lobbed another question without waiting for an answer to the first. "Is selling a possibility?"

"I guess anything is possible. I tell the board about every offer that comes in. My recommendation is they let me see the summer through before making a rash decision."

An engine rattled down the dirt road, sending clanking noises through the open office windows. Grace moved to the window.

"Looks like the cavalry has arrived."

He joined her. A conservation officer exited the cab of the truck, tugged down the brim of his hat, and headed toward the office. A news van pulled into the empty spot beside him, and a reporter jumped out and started taking footage in front of the long cylinder metal trap.

Grace laid her hand on his arm. "I meant what I said. I'll do whatever you need to help."

She continued to surprise him. "Thank you."

Grace turned back to the window and tipped her head to the side, fixated on the bear trap. "That's not what I pictured at all."

Kye fixed his eyes on Grace. "It's not what I expected either."

"Hey, Kate, any chance you could walk with me to the nurse's office so I can grab some painkillers?" Grace punched the speaker-phone option on her cell and rustled through her suitcase. Where were those pills?

"Sorry, I'm knee deep in arts and craft prep in the auditorium today. Where's your walking partner?"

Kye had insisted that all staff walked with partners until the bear was caught. The trouble was, Grace's partner was Kye, and he set her stomach rolling. Her bear get-up had been a joke, meant to break his tension. But the way he'd tiptoed around her feelings as if it mattered to him that he not mock her, had deeply touched her. It made her feel . . . well . . . she didn't exactly know what it made her feel, except restless. And that didn't help her headache.

She wasn't ready for these kinds of feelings.

"I didn't want to bother him when he's so concerned with trapping this bear." She emptied the last pocket in the suitcase. No painkillers. She had definitely forgotten to pack them. Considering all her preparations and first-aid training, it was a rookie mistake.

Kate laughed. "I think Kye would be *more than happy* to accompany you on a walk through the woods."

*Right.* Kate wasn't even in the room, but that didn't stop the heat from flooding Grace's face. "I'll figure it out. Thanks anyway." Grace disconnected and tried Debbie, but only got her voicemail. She debated calling Kye for about three seconds. Really, what were the chances of seeing the bear again?

Then again . . . the memories of its sheer

size made common sense prevail. She dialed his number. The phone went to his voice mail. *Great, now what?* She left a brief message. She finished unpacking, puttered around, and waited for him to call back. The pounding in her skull grew so bad she couldn't wait any longer.

Grabbing her bear spray and a stick, she moved onto the porch and peered into the woods. A quick check of her phone confirmed she hadn't missed a callback from Kye. What was taking him so long?

The trek to the nurse's office wasn't that far. Would it be so terrible if she walked it alone? She swatted a branch from her face and pushed through her headache, praying that her master key would open the door since the nurse wasn't scheduled to arrive for a few more days.

She probably should have waited for Kye to call back. Then again, she just wasn't ready to deal with all the mixed-up feelings he stirred. This summer was supposed to be about *her* program. About making amends for that fateful summer years ago.

Anyway, she had four lifeguards to run through the paces later today, and she needed this headache gone. She slowed as she approached the edge of the tree line and looked for signs of the bear.

The last she heard, the bear trap would be set between the woods and the dining hall. If she circled around, she should be able to get into the nurse's office via the dining hall's front door and avoid the hot zone. She jingled her keys in her pocket to ensure they were still there.

She spotted the man-sized metal cylinder that Kye and Ron, the conservation officer, had set up earlier. The sunlight glinted off the open trap door, signaling that the hunt was still on. A sugary-sweet scent wafted her way. What did they put in the bait bucket hanging from the hook inside the trap? She didn't care enough to go and find out. A shiver tiptoed down her spine. Medication. Then home.

The hairs on her neck bristled. She glanced around. Was Kye here watching? If so, why hadn't he come out and read her the riot act for walking alone? She fumbled for her keys.

The jingle seemed loud in the unusually quiet campground. Everyone was tucked away indoors until Kye gave the all clear. That's where she'd be too, as soon as she got something to take the edge off her pounding head.

She jumped at a rustling behind her and fumbled with the lock on the door. This was a bad idea. Really bad. Her clumsy fingers dropped the keys, and they clanked on the wooden porch, slipping between the widely spaced boards. Squatting, she strained to stretch her fingers far enough through the opening to snag them.

A low throaty warning rumbled behind her.

Blood roared through her ears as she peeked over her shoulder.

A black bear stood to its full height looking right at her. *Oh God, help!*

They stared each other down. The pain in her head quadrupled. She wasn't breathing. As she gasped, the bear charged.

A scream clawed from her toes all the way up her throat. She sprang up and shook the locked door. It wouldn't budge. She pounded on it, hoping against hope someone was inside. Nothing.

She spun around and waved her arms like a madwoman, trying to make herself look bigger than her slender frame. "Get back! Go away!" she hollered. The bear skidded to a stop and dropped to all fours only a few feet from the porch steps. She pressed her back against the locked door and whimpered, "Please, Lord, make it leave."

Co-workers, alerted by her shouts, yelled and banged on the glass from inside their buildings, and footsteps pounded from inside the dining hall. The chaos seemed to irk the bear even more.

*I'm gonna die.* Remembering her bear spray, Grace gripped it in sweaty palms, thankful Kye had insisted she trade her homemade recipe for the real deal when she left his office.

The bear stood again, sniffed the air, and twitched its nose in her direction. Grace held herself still but couldn't stop the violent trembling in her limbs. A crash sounded from another building, and the bear dropped again to all fours, swatting the ground with its front paw while blowing and snorting. Without turning her back to it, Grace crept across the porch and felt for the window, praying it was unlocked. Kate called to her from inside, and the door rattled as she worked the locks. The bear lifted its head, and a horrific growl pealed from its throat and drowned out Grace's screams.

A boom echoed through the grounds. Kye darted across the road, holding that useless shotgun armed with blanks. He racked the slide while he ran and fired again into the sky. Snorting and growling, the bear turned and swung its head from Kye to her.

"Get inside!" Kye roared and time slowed.

The bear's low rumble filled the air.

She dared not move. Or breathe.

"Now, Grace!"

Kate flung open the door from the inside, grabbed the back of Grace's T-shirt, and yanked her right off her feet.

"Kye!"

The bear started toward Kye.

Kye ripped off his hat and threw it at the bear, pinging it in the nose.

Grace tumbled into the dining hall, expecting Kye to race in behind her.

She was wrong.

# 6

*Eight feet to the door . . . Six . . . Five . . . No!*
A meaty paw slammed against his back and knocked him to the ground. His skull bounced off the dirt. The gun slipped from his hands. Kye curled his arms over his head and face. *Thank you, God, for getting Grace to safety.*

Bristly fur poked his arms. The bear nudged him with his snout. Hot breath dampened his skin.

Kye held his breath. He shoved down swelling panic that the bear didn't seem to be buying the act. He prayed like he had never prayed before in his life.

Another shot rang out.

The bear shifted, and coolness swept in.

"Roll, Kye!"

Kye rolled out from under the bear as Ron aimed the tranquilizer gun.

The gun whooshed, and the bear swayed.

Kye army-crawled toward Ron. Toward safety.

Ron stormed the teetering bear, gun aimed, another dart loaded, until he stood between Kye and the animal.

The bear thumped into the dirt.

Kye didn't move. Didn't breathe until Grace rolled him over and cupped his face in her hands. Then his breath came out in a rush.

"Are you OK?" She blurred before him. Her voice sounded a million miles away.

"Is he down?" He twisted around and groaned at the agony. The bear lay limp on his back, no more threatening than a rug in front of the fireplace. A dart stuck out from his hip. Kye fell against Grace. "Is he dead?"

The staff rushed in.

Eric leaned close and snapped a selfie with the bear. Crazy kid.

"Not dead. Just tranquilized." Grace's shaky smile stretched across her beautiful face.

She was safe. He did it. He saved her. He fell back onto the ground and covered his face with his hands.

"Are you OK?" Grace's tears dripped onto his cheeks, and her hands ran the length of his body checking for wounds.

He winced when her fingers snagged in

his hair. He must have banged his head pretty hard going down.

He pushed himself into a sitting position, willing his double vision to clear. He wiggled one arm and then the other one. Then he moved a foot, and the other one. His limbs all seemed to be attached to his body. *Thank you, Jesus.* "I'm fine. I think." His voice trembled. He didn't trust his legs yet, but he was alive.

Grace pressed close, and he inhaled her comforting scent. "Thank God you're OK." Her fingertips rested against his arms, as if she needed the physical contact with him.

He didn't let his mind linger on how good that contact felt.

Her body shuddered. "I can't believe you did that. That you ran out here. You saved me."

"Ah," Ron cleared his throat. "*I* actually saved you, and it would have been sooner if this bozo hadn't kept blocking my shot." He scowled at Kye. "You're one lucky guy. The bear will be out for about forty-five minutes. I'm going to get the truck and drive it back here. I'll round up a few guys to help load him in. This puppy weighs as much as two grown men."

Kye nodded. He deserved a dressing down for running out against Ron's instructions.

Ron might have a lot more to say to him after he loaded the animal into the cage.

Kye pushed himself up. Ready or not, his staff needed to see him on his feet. He gave the unconscious animal a wide berth and turned to the crowd. "Show's over, everyone. It's time to get back to work. We have a crew of campers arriving in less than two weeks."

They slowly left in groups of twos and threes chattering with excitement.

"And I don't want to see any of those pictures on Facebook!" he called after them. He reached out for Grace and snagged her hand, tugging her back to him. "What on earth were you doing out here alone?"

She dropped her eyes. "I needed some medication for a headache, and I knew I could get some from the nurse's room."

"You are not supposed to be walking alone. Why didn't you call me?"

"I did. It went to voice mail." She didn't lift her face, so he gently touched his fingers to her chin and lifted it for her. He should read her the riot act for not waiting for him, but her repentant eyes filled with tears and her bottom lip quivered. He tugged her into his arms. She pressed her face onto his shoulder.

He dipped his face into her hair and tasted

vanilla. His new favorite scent. "You must have called when I was on the line with another parent. They've been calling all day." His arms tightened around her, and it muffled her cries. He couldn't really blame her for not listening when he did the same thing. He had ignored Ron's calls and burst through the office doors with guns blazing when he saw the bear towering over Grace.

"I'm — so — sorry." It came out in broken hiccup-like sobs. "You could have been — killed. It would have been my fault. All my fault."

He circled his palm on her back as he held her. "It's OK. I'm OK. You're OK. The bear is gone. Everything will be fine."

He held her until Ron pulled up with his truck. Eric and Kaleb climbed out of the cab wearing smirks. Great. They'd seen him holding Grace in his arms. What were the chances they would view the scene as simple friends comforting one another?

"Let's get him loaded," Ron said. "We don't want this bad boy waking up before we've secured him."

Grace wiped her eyes. "Where are you taking him?"

"First, back to the municipal yard for measuring, collaring. Then we'll take him further north and release him by a nice

96

stream full of salmon. Hopefully, he'll never wander back."

Grace shuddered.

Ron grabbed a front paw. "Pick him up like this," he demonstrated the hold. "You," he nodded to Eric, "take the bottom foot. You," he nodded to Kaleb, "the other front paw."

Kye grabbed the remaining paw. The bear lay on his back, snout up, eyes open.

Kye's mouth went dry. His hands sweated as he held the paw, still warm from their encounter. A steady breath didn't slow his racing pulse.

"OK, let's lift and swing on the count of three," said Ron.

Suddenly, the bear shook his head, let out a sharp snort, and sprayed saliva.

Grace yelped. The guys dropped the feet and scrambled backwards.

Ron chuckled. "It's just a reflex. Happens all the time. You yahoos aren't taking selfies now, are you?"

Eric snorted.

"A heads-up would have been nice." Kye grabbed the hind paw again with the same confidence he might feel handling venomous snakes.

"One, two, three!" They heaved the bear into the cage. Kye shook Ron's hand, and

Ron leaned in. "I found some questionable things in the woods. Now you're a smart man, so I doubt you put them there, but it looks like someone had been trying to lure a bear here on purpose."

What?

Ron tipped his hat and shot a look toward Eric and Kaleb, who were still snapping pictures. He handed him a card. "Call me."

Eric and Kaleb snapped pictures of the retreating vehicle. Kye wondered what other pictures they had.

He rubbed his forehead. "These pics will be plastered all over social media, won't they?"

"I'll comment and make sure you come off like a hero." Grace nudged him with her shoulder. "We won't let your ego take a hit."

Except his ego wasn't the problem. Bad press made parents pull their kids, and pictures without context might give the staff — and Grace — the wrong idea about him and her.

Not to mention that he seriously doubted his ability to handle a permanent reminder of how close he'd come to losing Grace today. And that did crazy things to his heart.

Eric and Kaleb wandered away clicking on their phones, but the wind carried their voices back. "How much do you want to bet boss-man fires Grace?"

"No way," said Kaleb. "Didn't you see them when we pulled up? A dude can't fire his girlfriend. That's suicide."

"That ain't right, man. If it were us, we'd be gone."

Kye glanced over at Grace. Her questioning gaze burned into his mind. Had she heard Eric and Kaleb, or had she heard Ron?

Kye pinched the bridge of his nose and briefly squeezed his eyes shut. *Lord, give me patience.*

Graham sat across from his desk begging for Grace's job. "She needs this, Kye. I can't say it enough."

*Yes, you can.*

A short night's sleep did little to relieve the pounding in Kye's skull. He spent half the night searching for a loophole that would allow him to keep Grace on staff and the other half trying not to dwell on why he wanted her there. He massaged his temples. Where was Judy with his coffee? If he ever needed a caffeine pick-me-up, it was now.

He forced his attention back to Graham. "If it were anyone else —"

"Excuse me," Judy interrupted from the door. "Here's your coffee, Kye." She crossed the room and placed a steaming mug on Kye's desk before turning to Graham. "Are you sure I can't get you anything?"

"No, thanks. I'll be leaving shortly."

"Thank you, Judy." Kye slid his coffee mug closer and breathed in the warm, pungent steam.

Judy closed the door behind her.

"Don't fire her," Graham repeated. "You're what Grace needs."

*What was that supposed to mean?*

Kye sidestepped the demand. Maintaining the balance between giving the locals a voice and requesting they respect his final authority required a skill he sorely lacked on minimal sleep.

"What makes you think her job is in jeopardy?"

Graham rubbed his jaw with his finger and thumb and gave a ridiculous look. "If you're even half the businessman the board insisted you were when they brought you in, you'd have to be considering it. She disobeyed a direct order."

He was a businessman who spent the night looking for a way around the rules. What did that say about him?

"You understand that I cannot speak with you about an employee's future with this camp, even if she is your stepdaughter." He locked eyes with Graham. They stared each other down. Kye wouldn't be the first to speak, nor would he give way.

"Grace is exactly what an extreme sports camp needs," Graham finally spoke. "She has grit and determination. She's a survivor."

An image of Grace facing the bear flashed in his mind. She was a survivor all right.

"She does whatever it takes to get the job done," Graham pressed.

"Including disregard orders?"

"Invite her to test some of the equipment. Let her show you what she's made of."

Kye nearly spit his coffee across the desk at the man. Was he insane? Invite the woman who, in no uncertain terms, expressed her complete disapproval of his program and ignored his orders?

"Grace and I have scheduled a meeting to discuss what happened. She can fill you in on our discussion afterwards, if she chooses."

"Humor an old man. Ask."

After Graham left, Kye rolled the idea around in his mind. He'd love to see Grace enjoy the thrilling activities planned for camp. He'd love nothing more than to spend the day testing equipment with Grace. Probably too much.

He pushed aside the niggling thought that lately she had filled his thoughts far too much.

He wasn't attracted to her. OK, maybe a little. She oozed an odd balance of strength and fear that he couldn't figure out. It was both frustrating and, well, attractive. Whether he was really drawn to her or simply challenged by her, he had yet to decide.

But either way, she broke the rules, and he had to address it before Eric and Kaleb spread their theory for why he let her off the hook.

He caught a whiff of vanilla.

"Hi." Her voice broke the silence.

His eyes snapped open.

"How's the headache?" Grace lingered in the doorway with a concerned wrinkle in her brow.

"I've been better." He waved her into the room. "Thanks for coming in to see me."

She stepped in but stayed close to the door.

"We need to talk about yesterday."

Her eyebrows shot up, and her eyes widened. She'd clearly heard the guys debating her job security. It was written all over her face.

He pressed his lips together. "You openly

disobeyed a rule I put in place for your safety."

Her shoulders sagged, and her gaze dropped to the floor. "I'm sorry."

He inhaled deeply hoping the aroma of coffee beans would overpower her vanilla.

No luck. He pushed the mug away.

"Somehow, considering all your lobbying against my camp ideas, you were the last staffer I expected to have to discipline over safety rules." And the fact she was the one caught by the bear meant she likely wasn't the one trying to lure him to the camp, or the source of threats against him.

She studied the floor as if something more amazing was happening on the carpet.

"Come on, Grace. I'm going to need more from you. If you were anyone else, you'd already be fired."

Her chin quivered, but she lifted it high. She firmed it and schooled her expression, but not before fear flashed through her eyes.

Why hadn't he fired her? He shoved the thought away. He didn't want to consider the reasons or implications of his leniency.

When she finally spoke, her words came out wooden and emotionless. "I understand if you need to let me go. I know saying I tried to get in touch with you is not good enough."

She shifted her weight to her other foot and blinked repeatedly.

*Oh Lord, please don't let her cry!* He didn't want her to cry. He just wanted her to understand the seriousness of her decision.

She chewed her lip, waiting.

She should be uncomfortable. Wondering if she still had a job for a half-second didn't even come close to his discomfort underneath that bear or how uncomfortable Eric and Kaleb's conclusions would be if she stayed on staff.

He leaned back in his chair until it tilted backwards. "What's really going on here?"

She blinked.

"The Grace who champions ultimate safety measures for the campers is not the same Grace who walked through the woods alone. Which one is real? Which girl have I hired?"

Her face drained to a pasty white.

Kye cocked his head to the side. Why did his questions seem to make her so uncomfortable? "You swim to Moshe Island alone. You ignore rules meant for your protection. Then, you squawk about unsafe camp conditions and risky outings for the children." He folded his arms across his chest.

Grace sighed and moved toward the chair in front of his desk. She hesitated only a minute before sitting down as if sitting committed her to a course of action she wasn't fully convinced she should take.

"I don't really know how to explain it except to say that when it comes to myself, I feel quite capable." She snatched a quick look at him then bounced her eyes away. "Usually."

At least she had the good manners to look sheepish. She hadn't done a very good job of taking care of herself yesterday.

"If I could only fire the foolish Grace, I would."

Her panicked eyes thrust a dagger in his gut.

She deflated.

Her quiet submission twisted the knife.

"But," he said softly, "I kind of like the brave Grace, despite the trouble she causes."

Her quivering lips turned into a faint smile.

A surge of pleasure flooded him. He liked making her smile. He cleared his throat and stacked the papers on his desk into a neat pile. "So let's see if I've got this figured out. You're OK taking risks yourself, but you need to protect the campers by removing all danger?"

"They're just kids, Kye. They have no clue how far-reaching consequences can be. No real concept of mortality. They believe nothing can ever hurt them until it does. I don't want one of them to have to live with regret like —" She snapped her mouth closed and turned away.

Her impassioned speech clicked everything into place. Someone she cared about had been hurt, and she still carried the guilt. That's why she enjoyed adventure, liked swimming alone, but hated the idea of this camp.

She looked at her hands twisting in her lap. "If I get hurt, it only hurts me. I can handle that."

"Grace," he leaned onto his elbows daring her to maintain eye contact. "If you got hurt on my watch, it would hurt *me.* This isn't just about you."

A deep pink rose in her cheeks, creating a pretty flush of innocence. He steeled himself against the urge to comfort her. Annette had soured his faith. She also once looked innocent and pure, but then he'd discovered she'd been manipulating him the entire time.

Still, his heart thudded against his ribs like he'd free-fallen from a cliff face without a safety harness. *Get a grip!*

"As far as the kids go, I'd never let you or anyone else take unnecessary risks just for the thrill."

She flicked her gaze to his, and the raw pain in her eyes nearly undid him. "I believe it," she whispered.

He sat back and held her gaze until she looked away.

"Prove it," he said softly.

"What?" Her body snapped to attention.

"The equipment arrives today. Help me set it up. And later, once we get the ropes and anchors set up for rock climbing, join me in testing it out."

Her neutral expression camouflaged her thoughts. "Aren't the guys supposed to do that?"

"Yeah, but they're busy fixing up what the bear wrecked inside the dining hall." A soundtrack of hammering and saws played in the background. Shame twinged his gut. Mentioning the b-word was dirty pool. She'd feel obligated. "Come rock climbing with me. No kids. No risk. Just you and me."

Quiet.

"Let me see which Grace is working for Camp Moshe. The brave one, who can handle anything thrown her way, the kind of staffer I need on my team, or the timid one, hedging her bets and causing trouble."

She studied him for a half beat. "OK."

Her concession came so softly it took a

second to register.

But before he could celebrate victory, an impish glint lit her eyes. "On one condition."

"What's that?"

"You swim with me tomorrow morning at sunrise."

"Deal." He extended his hand, and they shook on it. Only . . . if he got what he wanted, why did he suddenly feel like he'd been played?

# 7

Grace glanced at her watch again. Kye was late.

Not even the brilliant early-morning sunshine could lighten the rock settling in her gut. Did he forget? Did he choose not to come? Or did her ping-ponging between following the safety measures and disregarding the rules seal her fate before she could prove herself? She pushed the questions down. It wasn't like she could tell him about her sister and dad. He didn't need another reason to fire her. He needed a reason to keep her.

The stiff breeze and the cloudless sky created a perfect morning to swim. What did she care if he pulled a no-show and she swam alone? She had nothing to prove. If he had planned to fire her, he would have done it yesterday.

But he didn't. He put her on probation instead.

And she still couldn't figure out why.

She shoved that down as well. She had enough to worry about launching Water Survival for Non-Swimmers. This summer would determine if she received the provincial funding she needed to do a province-wide launch. She didn't have time to stress over Kye's motivation. *Thank you, God for second chances.*

She'd show Kye that she was an asset to his program, someone not easily replaced, and someone he wanted on staff. She'd affirm his inclination to give her another chance.

But to do any of that, he had to show up.

She tapped her foot. Each passing minute cooled her hope. What kind of employer failed to keep his word?

A rustling behind her announced his arrival a half-beat before he spoke.

"Sorry, I'm late." He jogged to her side, panting from his sprint. "Slept through my alarm."

"Aren't you a runner?" If he huffed this much just jogging in from the cabins, the swim would kill him. Maybe this wasn't such a good idea.

"Yeah, distance, not sprint." He bent at the waist and wheezed in a breath.

Her heart did one of those odd flip-flop things.

*Get a grip, girl! This is your boss.*

His muscular arms and tanned skin spiked her resting heart rate. She shook it off. She'd had her share of fine-looking men try to impress her with their physique. Kye, on the other hand, appeared oblivious to his good looks and charm. That trait grew more and more attractive each passing day. "I was just heading in. Ready?"

"Without me? I'm wounded!" He grabbed at his chest and feigned heart-brokenness, melting her earlier irritation with a sleepy smile.

She playfully swatted at his arm, dropped her terrycloth swim wrap, and waded in. When the water reached her ankles, she stopped and tossed her best casual look over her shoulder. She wasn't about to let the cold water bother her any more than his near no-show had. "Coming?"

He kicked off his shoes and tugged off his shirt.

She averted her eyes. Why did she invite him to swim?

"What's the plan?" He matched her step for step into the water and followed her gaze settling on the gorgeous sunrise.

She couldn't tell him she wanted him on

her turf so she could knock his socks off with her skill. "Ah, the plan is to get you wet."

He looked at his feet under a foot of clear water. "Check."

She socked his arm and knocked him off-balance, sending him splashing onto his backside.

"I meant more wet."

He raised his dripping arms, and his dimpled cheek flashed. "Mission accomplished."

She turned toward the sunrise and waded deeper. Why did heat flood her face every time he showed that dimple? What chance did she have that he'd think it was an early-season sunburn? "What kind of skill do you have?"

He pushed a bit of water her way and steadied himself, stepping close. Really close. She had to tilt her head to look up at him.

His gaze flitted to her lips, then back to her eyes, then back to her lips, where they lingered.

For a crazy half-second, she anticipated a kiss. Would he? Would she? The lapping waves coaxed her closer.

"I used to swim in high school on the team." He bent his knees and dipped himself into the lake to mid-chest and then popped back up.

A flash of disappointment rushed over their lost moment of . . . of whatever that was.

She lifted an unimpressed brow. "Lake swimming is very different than pool swimming. I usually go out to Moshe Island and back, but that might be a bit far if you're not used to the pull of the lake." She backed into deeper water and beckoned him with the crook of her finger. "Let's start with a leisurely swim parallel to shore and see how you do."

Kye shot a look of interest toward the island and then conceded. "You're the master."

She grinned. She liked the sound of that.

When he dipped his head in a false submissive bow, she grabbed his shoulders and shoved him under the water. Then, she took off with a shriek.

He came up coughing and laughing. "You better swim!"

She stroked hard and fast. His fingers brushed her ankle but never caught hold. She welcomed his surprising ability. A hard scissor kick sent a wall of water behind her.

A small part of her wanted to work him harder than he expected. To see her as more than a counselor or camp liability. She wanted him to view her as a valued member of his team. She appreciated this second chance and wasn't going to blow it. She *needed* him to acknowledge her capabilities.

Grace led the way to the open water, noting his pace slightly behind her. As they swam parallel to the shore with the current, she counted strokes and took her cue from the beautiful morning. *The heavens are telling of the glory of God, and the sky above proclaims his handiwork, Psalms 19:1.*

Her chest puffed a bit as he lagged.

Maybe she should recite Proverbs 16:18? *Pride goes before destruction. A haughty spirit before a fall.*

She stopped mid-lake and treaded.

"How are you doing?"

He panted. "Tired."

His shallow breaths and sloppy arms indicated fatigue but not exhaustion. However, he did just survive a bear attack. Maybe she should take it easy on the poor guy. "Ready to turn back?"

He huffed. "Only if you are." *Typical macho man.*

He needed a rest, even if he wasn't ready to admit it. They rode the rolling waves sent their way from the early morning boaters and enjoyed a breather. She made sure they stayed within reach of a sandbar in case he needed it, and stayed far from the submerged rocks scattered throughout the area.

"That's the rock the kids will climb." Kye pointed to an escarpment that angled out over the water.

The enormous rock rose high, almost completely vertical.

He pointed at another section where a chuck of rock jutted out like a natural diving board over the lake. "And they'll jump from that spot."

She bit her tongue. She'd already voiced her thoughts about the camp. Harping on it wouldn't win her any probation points. And thankfully, that point of the lake was exceptionally deep and without the treacherous hidden boulders that littered the shallower areas.

"Hey, it's Jeremy." She nodded toward a dock where Jeremy sat with her mother's dog, Bisket.

"Jeremy." Kye squinted. "And a dog?"

"Yup. It's my mom's dog." She changed direction and swam toward them, stopping a little way from the dock and treading. She waved at Jeremy. "Can Bisket come in?"

"Sure." He unleashed her.

"Bisket! Come on, girl. Come on!"

Bisket leapt into the lake and paddled toward Grace. But after a few feet, Bisket's head slipped under the water and didn't resurface.

"Bisket!" Jeremy jumped to his feet. "Something's wrong!"

Grace took off toward the dog, pausing long enough to scan the surface.

"There." Kye pointed.

Surprised at his ability to keep up, Grace followed his direction and dove under the waves. Her foot feathered against something odd, and she kicked it away. She surfaced close to Bisket who had managed to stretch her neck and push her nose above water. "Bisket!"

At the sound of her name, the dog swiped out a panicked paw. Her nails raked Grace's arm, drawing blood.

Grace's hand caught on a downward stroke and snagged as if something had wrapped silky tentacles around her wrist. She grabbed Bisket and yanked up. The hold on her wrist tightened. Whatever hindered Bisket now had her!

She sucked in a breath and dove under the water. She ignored the throbbing of her arm and snapped a string binding her to the dog with her teeth just as Kye grabbed Bisket by the scruff of her neck and aimed for the shore.

"Wait! She's still caught in some string!" She dove under and untangled the rest of the string from Bisket's legs and herself. A less experienced swimmer could have drowned. Bile rose in her throat, and she swallowed hard.

She freed the dog, and the tension on the string instantly released. She snagged another quick breath and dove to investigate, remaining a safe distance from the clear string rolling and curling with the waves.

Finally, she surfaced.

Kye treaded nearby, holding Bisket. Finding him waiting for her did funny things to her heart.

Kye's muscles rippled. Adrenaline must have overpowered his fatigue because he easily dragged the dog onto the beach and put her down. This time she struggled to keep up with him.

Grace hit the sand a few footsteps behind and applied pressure to her wound with her hand. So much for showing off for the boss-man.

"Are you hurt?" With an eye on the panting dog, Kye tenderly investigated her upper arm. It slowly wept red between her fingers.

"Only my pride."

He peeled her fingers away from the wound and then quickly pressed them back and applied more pressure with his hand. "We need to get you back to camp."

"Bisket! Bisket!" Jeremy pounded his way toward them. "What had her all tangled up? I couldn't see anything in the water."

Kye nudged the boy, "How about you give your sister your shirt so I can wrap her cut?"

Jeremy's eyes widened finally noticing her arm.

"Are you OK?" He ripped off his T-shirt and handed it to Kye.

Kye wrapped it around her tricep, cinching it a little tighter than comfortable.

She winced.

His hands stilled, and his gaze found hers. "Grace?"

"I'm fine." She shimmied out of his hold.

"Is Bisket OK?" Jeremy squatted beside the dog resting on the sand. Her tongue lolled as she panted hard.

"She'll be fine." Grace assured him. "There was a mess of netting under the surface. It's nearly clear, so it's hard to see." She looked at Kye. "If a child got into that, they could drown."

"Have you ever found netting in the lake before?"

"No. And Debbie and I already checked

118

this spot for safety concerns, and there wasn't any. This is new."

"You'll have to redo all your safety checks to ensure the other swimming spots haven't been compromised."

She stifled a sigh. He probably thought she just missed the net, but it wasn't there before. She knew it. She held her words behind clenched teeth and forced a smile. "I'll get Debbie on it as soon as we return to camp."

Jeremy pounced on the opportunity to pepper Kye with question after question about cliff jumping and rock climbing. Kye held out his hand to stem the flow.

"We'd better head back to camp. Your sister can't swim until we bandage that cut," Kye motioned to Grace's upper arm, "and it's a long way around the lake on foot. So let's get started."

She took the leash from Jeremy and motioned for the boys to walk ahead. She latched Bisket on and followed.

Jeremy's energy vibrated. "You were awesome, Kye. The way you pulled Bisket in and dropped her on the sand, then used my shirt to fix Grace's arm. You're like MacGyver or Superman."

Grace narrowed her eyes. Traitor.

Kye deflected Jeremy's adoration, but it

didn't change that he'd been cast in the role of hero.

It had become a pattern of sorts. An irritating one. And she was bad luck for heroes.

She caused Kye to be nearly mauled to death by a bear, and her reckless childhood broke her family.

Yup. She was kryptonite to heroes.

"I'm sure it's fine." Grace shrugged off Kye's concern. Something about the gentle way he guided her to a seat put her on edge. She didn't need a hero.

"This might hurt a little." Kye squeezed some antibiotic ointment onto his gloved finger and dabbed her wound.

His fingers grazed her skin, and she flinched.

Kye hesitated, his eyes flicking to hers. He leaned in closer and re-inspected the scrape.

Her instinctive response had far more to do with his warm fingers on her skin than the cut, but she couldn't tell him that. Why did the man have to be so good looking? His clean, woodsy aftershave filled the small nurse's office.

She gripped the lip of her chair. "It's not that bad," she insisted. "It just stings a bit."

Seemingly satisfied, he finished treating

120

her wound and straightened. Coolness swept between them, and she instantly missed the heat of the charged air.

"If Bisket hadn't scratched you in such an awkward spot for soap and water, you could have managed without me." Kye put the medicated ointment away.

As much as she wanted to manage without him — needed to manage without him — a small part of her enjoyed his tender attention. Maybe too much. She hopped off the chair. "So we're done?"

He pulled out a bandage from the first aid kit and ripped it open. "Just about." Kye pressed the bandage on her arm and smiled. "There. All better."

She caught her breath. Her wound might be better, but what about the rest of her? She edged toward the door, pasting a smile on her face. "Next time the camp nurse will be here, and you won't have to play doctor." She was almost out the door. Two more steps, one —

He pulled off the latex gloves and tossed them in the garbage can. "She doesn't arrive for two more days. So no more injuries, OK?"

She blushed. "Maybe we should postpone rock climbing together." She stopped in the doorway, as a hopeful smile twitched the corners of her lips. Bisket's panicked attack might prove to be helpful after all.

"This isn't bad enough to cancel that," he laughed. He turned to put the rest of the first aid supplies away and asked over his shoulder, "So, how do you think the netting got there?"

Her body sagged. "I don't know. I swam there two days ago, and the water was clear of debris."

"Hmm."

That was it? A grunt? Kye looked like he had some strong feelings about what happened, but she couldn't make him share them. "Debbie is already removing it, and she'll double check the other areas I had previously cleared." She knew she was prattling. What if he thought negligence on her part had missed this?

He nodded. "Let me know what you find. Hey, did I hear right? Are you giving Jeremy private lessons in the lake?"

Grace froze. Jeremy had maintained a streak of conversation as they walked around the lake back to camp. She had hoped Kye hadn't heard that part. She put a hand to her stomach to stop the rising tide of panic. "I'm doing it on my own time, Kye. After work." The words tumbled out.

She had to teach these lessons to Jeremy.

*Please God, don't make me give them up.*

Concern flooded Kye's face. "You've gone completely white." He pulled her back into the room and guided her to the sofa. "Maybe there's more to that scratch than we thought."

Her mind raced for a response that could explain away her panic. She couldn't tell him why she was teaching Jeremy. Not when she was on probation.

"So what are you teaching him? I thought he'd be a pretty good swimmer considering he's your half-brother and all." He sat down across from her and leaned forward.

"Some tips to help in the lake water. Things he wouldn't know from a pool." She lifted a shoulder in an awkward shrug.

His eyes drilled into hers.

Was he seeing more than she wanted?

"Isn't he here every summer?"

"Yeah, but Mom doesn't let him swim too much. Uh, coffee?" Grace nodded toward the coffee machine and the selection of flavored pods. She wasn't much of a coffee drinker, but anything sounded better than sitting near to Kye and letting him pick apart her family secrets.

"I'll get it. You sit." Kye looked over the selection. "You like salted caramel, right?"

Grace nodded and closed her eyes. Pleasure that he not only noticed her morning beverage choice, but also remembered it, zipped through her. The machine whirred a promising hum and one by one she willed her tense muscles to relax.

"So why doesn't your mom let Jeremy swim in the lake?"

She shifted, and carefully chose her words. "Jeremy frequently underestimates the lake. But, like the ocean, a lake can be wild and unpredictable. The best swimmer respects the water, never ever believes himself to be stronger." She swallowed past the lump forming in her throat. If she could only go back in time and learn that herself.

He wrinkled his forehead, clearly not satisfied. He handed her the coffee. "So your mother doesn't like him swimming, but you are an exceptional teacher. What gives?"

She stalled and sipped her drink. "You heard her that day on the beach, didn't you, questioning my ability?"

"I did." Compassion filled his gaze.

She broke eye contact and bit her lip. Several uncomfortable seconds passed.

"Look, I could pretend to be oblivious to whatever is going on here, but that wouldn't make me a very good friend."

Grace's breath caught in her throat. *Pretend.*

"Grace?" Kye's expression cut through her heart.

She had to tell him. She rubbed at a building headache.

In some ways, it would have been easier if someone had already told him. Her gut twisted against the pity that would inevitably fill his eyes. She may not know what she wanted from Kye, but she knew it wasn't pity.

"Did something happen?" Kye's tender voice broke through her fog. "Are you afraid?"

She shook her head. A drop of coffee sloshed over the edge of her mug.

"Then why are your hands trembling?" He took her mug from her hands and set it on the table. He then unfolded a heavy blanket draped over the back of the sofa and spread it over her legs. He rested his weight on his forearms and knees eliminating some of the space between them.

She inhaled sharply and held onto his scent. The lingering taste of salted caramel coffee catapulted her back in time to that hot summer day on the salty Caribbean ocean. The day her life changed forever.

She dropped her eyes and blinked against the building tears.

Kye squeezed her hands.

When did he take her hands? She tugged them away and wrapped them around her middle.

"My Dad and sister . . ." The explanation tangled in her throat. She swallowed and started again. "They died when I was young. They drowned in the ocean." Her voice dropped to a whisper.

"Oh." The single word came out as a guttural groan. "I'm so sorry." He placed a hand on her knee.

Hot tears spilled over and splashed down before she could blink them away. She pinched her eyes shut tighter. She wouldn't cry. Not here. Not with him. "I tried to save them." Her ragged breathing filled the room. Her heart thundered in her ears. Once she spilled out the story, there was no putting it back. It would change things. It always changed things.

"Grace," he tipped up her chin with two fingers and forced eye contact. "Do you feel responsible?"

She searched his face. Her mother had blamed her. That's why she didn't fully trust her with Jeremy. But Kye couldn't know that. "I was the stronger swimmer, but we got caught in a riptide and I —" her voice caught, "I couldn't save Becky." It came out in a whisper so soft, she wasn't sure he

126

heard her.

His eyes dampened. "How old were you?"

"Eleven." Jeremy was almost eleven. "I left her. Alone." Her voice cracked, and there was no way to stop the flow of tears now.

Just like there were no words to convey what really occurred that day.

Kye's chair groaned as he moved. His weight on the sofa shifted Grace toward him, jolting her from her memory. Thigh to thigh, heat radiated from him. He flipped her hand over and rubbed soft circles into the palm as if it were the most natural thing in the world. He waited. Quiet. Unassuming. Patient.

She took in another shaky breath. "When I made it back to the boat, Mom was on the radio with the Coast Guard. Dad pulled me up. When Becky couldn't make it to the boat, Dad dove in. Mom dropped the radio and started screaming because he wasn't a great swimmer. I tried throwing the life preserver, but the waves rolled it away. When Dad finally reached Becky, she climbed up on top of him, pushing him under in her panic to stay above water."

Grace fixated on a tiny scratch on the wall just above Kye's shoulder. "That's when Mom had to hold me back." She didn't notice that she traced the scar her mother's nails had carved into her wrist until Kye's hand settled on top of hers. "We threw everything we had to them, reached out with our arms, oars, anything. We tried to steer the boat around. Nothing worked."

She didn't explain what it was like to watch them slip under the surface that last time and sink down into their inky grave. She didn't voice her devastation at the Coast Guard arriving five minutes too late, how they stood on the boat for hours, refusing to leave, watching that last spot where her dad and sister fought for breath. She couldn't put that into words because there were no words.

Kye pulled her into his arms, his strength cradling her sorrow. His words pressed to her hair. "You were a child. It wasn't your fault."

She jerked herself back. "Yes, it was. I was the one who wanted to swim in the ocean. I was the one who went out further than I should. We never would have been caught in that riptide if we'd stayed close to shore." She rubbed a fist over her eyes, scraping away the tears.

"Becky followed me. I knew she wasn't a strong swimmer. I knew it, Kye." She looked him in the eye. "I was a selfish kid who thought nothing bad would ever happen."

Her voice cracked. "And my dad and sister paid for it."

"And now you dedicate your life to protecting kids."

She nodded and sniffed. "Your camp ideas sound fun, for someone like me, old enough to count the cost of my choices. But if a child is hurt —"

"Oh, Grace." He pulled her in close again. "It wouldn't be your fault. Surely the Coast Guard or friend told you —"

"I spent years talking with a counselor, but no one has ever been able to explain why God let this happen."

She steeled herself against Kye's pained expression, the same one others wore before offering some weak platitude about God's sovereignty or His ability to use loss for good. All the right theology in the world didn't take the pain away.

"I think smarter people than us have wrestled with these types of questions and come up empty."

She blinked at his unexpected response.

"The world is broken. Broken by sin, devastated by death. Living here hurts."

She exhaled. He knew everything and didn't run away. He didn't try to fix her. And her questions about God didn't intimidate him. He acknowledged her pain and let her feel it.

They sat quietly, side by side, not touching, not speaking, just quiet and comfortable until the camp truck rumbled to a stop outside the open window. Kaleb and Eric spilled out and started unloading boxes. After a minute, Bobby joined them. Their chatter wafted back through the screened window that perfectly framed Kye and Grace sitting on the cozy couch.

Kye stood up a little too quickly.

Was he embarrassed? Had she crossed some sort of line?

"Looks like the equipment is here." Kye mussed his hair with his hand. His unnatural fidgeting and his quick glances between her and the guys solidified it. She had blurred the employee/employer lines, and he didn't like it.

## 8

First, someone lured a bear to the camp, and then they deposited a fish net in the lake? It was beginning to look like whoever had been threatening him was making good on his promise to hurt someone. Grace could have drowned today. Kye pounded a nail into the pre-drilled slot on a slide.

Something had shifted between them after Grace unburdened her heart. Kye couldn't put his finger on it. It was like a wall erected, and no matter what he did he couldn't scale it. Grace hadn't been the same since they left the nurse's office to help unload the sporting equipment onto the beach. Sure, she did everything with a smile, made helpful suggestions, and worked without complaint. But, her sparkle was gone. Surprisingly, he realized he'd do almost anything to get it back.

"How's this layout?" Bobby took a few steps back from the extreme obstacle course they had laid out for the kids. "It'll have whipped cream or sudsy water on the slide, and the beam will extend over the lake. That way the loser falls into the water."

The primary-colored padded rings, poles, and beams looked kid friendly enough, but would anyone be able to do it?

Kye glanced toward Grace, who had wandered to the refreshment table Kate had set up with bottled water and snacks. She chatted with Kate, not looking his way.

"It looks good," Kye replied.

"The course or the girl?" Bobby nudged Kye's arm and nodded toward Grace. Then he grabbed Kye's shoulders and pivoted him. "The course is this way."

Kye's face heated, and he shrugged out of Bobby's hands. "I know. I saw it." If seeing him and Grace in the nurse's office wasn't enough to stir the gossip pot, this sure would.

"It's great," Kye affirmed. "Hard — but good."

"Do you think it's too hard?" Kaleb joined the conversation and scratched his head.

Another glance at Grace confirmed she was still ignoring him in that intentional way all women seemed to have mastered.

"There's only one way to find out." Kye took off in a sprint. Desperate times called for desperate measures.

"Wait, Kye —"

Kye ran full speed toward the slide. He stole a sideways look and satisfaction rose. Grace watched. He upped his pace.

Two steps up the slide and it shifted under his feet. No! The lip slipped, dropping Kye and the slide three feet into the sand. His arms shot out to break his fall, and his face exploded against the yellow plastic hump halfway up the slide.

He rolled over, groaning. Kaleb, Bobby, Grace, and Kate hovered over him. How did they get here so fast?

He sat up and felt liquid running from his nostrils. He pressed the hem of his T-shirt against his nose. "It's not that bad," he insisted, but it came out all muffled from behind his bunched-up T-shirt. The shirt quickly deepened to a dark shade of red, darkening with every passing second.

"I'm taking you to Emergency," Grace announced.

Her insistence both warmed and humiliated him. "You don't have to do that —"

"Yes, I do." She smiled, but it didn't quite wipe the worry from her eyes. "You blacked out for a few seconds."

That explained their lightning speed reaching him.

Her soft hands prodded his body as she checked him for other injuries. "I'm fine," he repeated.

"What were you thinking running up the slide before anyone tested it? You gotta slow down and stop doing everything at full speed." She slid her eyes over his, and he squirmed under her scrutiny. He couldn't very well explain that his lack of focus was her fault.

"I can't believe you did that." Kaleb punched Kye on the shoulder. "I tried to call you back, but you were gone." His mocking laughter multiplied Kye's discomfort. This was not the way he wanted to get Grace's attention.

"Let's go." Grace hoisted him up.

Kye tipped his head back and pinched the bridge of his nose to slow the flow of blood. There was so much blood.

He groaned every time her sedan hit a bump in the road. The pain zipping through his sinus tract kept pace with the argument he had with himself inside his head.

What had he thought? That running up the slide would magically transport them back into the comfortable intimacy they enjoyed in the nurse's office? The minute her walls shot back up, he'd wanted to tear them down. He'd needed to do something drastic and coax out a smile. Mission accomplished. His totally stupid stunt didn't merely break the ice between them. It broke his nose. And she noticed him all right. It was hard to miss the guy bleeding all over the obstacle course.

"We're almost there." Grace said as she pulled into the parking lot.

"Good." Kye coughed. Excess blood seeped through the saturated fabric and over his fingers, which were now sticky and wet.

"Tamera is meeting us at admitting."

"You called my mother? When?"

"When Bobby was helping you into the car." She leveled a look his way. "I'd want to know if my son was hurt." Grace parked the car and turned off the engine.

"Since when is she on your speed dial?"

"Since you cancelled our Sunday lunch. I looked her up and called to apologize. We've chatted a few times since." She got out of the car and came around to his side to help him out.

"You talk to my mother?"

"Yeah. Why not?" The double doors leading into the hospital slid open.

Of course. It was all starting to make sense. His mother had recently paused the get-married-and-settle-down speech. He had hoped it was because she was starting to respect his decisions. Turns out she was working the system from another angle. He should have known.

The minute they stepped into the room, his mother rushed him. "Malachi Campton! What were you thinking?"

"Hi, Mom." He shot Grace a *see-what-you-did* look.

Grace smiled.

"Don't *Mom* me. This is serious. You know what happens when you injure your nose. Ever since that time you fell out of the tree when you were six, you've had to get it cauterized to stop the bleeding."

"Let it go." Kye clenched his teeth and added an aching jaw to his list of ailments.

"I brought you a clean shirt." His mom sighed and looked pointedly at Grace, who quickly looked away. "If you had a nice woman and settled down, she could bring you clean shirts instead of me."

Grace seemed to be trying to hide a grin. She was enjoying this far too much.

His cell phone chirped. Saved by the bell. "Gotta take this, Mom. Can you register me?" He pushed his mother into the direction of the admitting nurse and then wandered through the double doors into the parking lot. "Hello?"

"You enjoying camp?" his boss asked.

"Yeah, it's been fun." Maybe if he kept his answers short, his boss wouldn't notice him gagging on blood?

"Not too much fun, I hope."

*Not unless you count threatening notes, bear attacks, suspicious wire in the lake, and hospital visits as fun.* He shifted the wad of tissues he'd grabbed from the waiting room to better stem the flow of blood. "What's up?"

"We have your next job lined up. A toy company in Phoenix needs some help re-branding their name. It starts September tenth."

"Count me in." He glanced through the large waiting room windows and did a double take. Grace had her hands over his mother's, their heads bowed, praying. *For him?* He disconnected the call, a second before registering that his boss had still been talking. What more was there to say? He said he'd be there.

His heart did a funny roll in his chest as he watched Grace's lips move, her eyes scrunched in earnestness. And for the first time, the idea of rushing to the next fix didn't hold much appeal.

Thankfully, the quiet ER enabled the admitting nurse to usher him into a room as soon as he returned. His mother followed him into the space sectioned off into four private areas by curtains. The nurse instructed Kye to sit on the examining bed, and then she pulled the curtain shut offering some semblance of privacy. A long sigh escaped him.

"That sounds like it hurts." A man in a white lab coat yanked back the curtain and strode to the bedside.

"It does," Kye read his name tag. "Doctor Brown."

"So how did it happen?" Doctor Brown shone a penlight into each one of Kye's eyes. He gently pressed and prodded his face.

"I ran an obstacle course." Kye flashed his mother a warning glare when her mouth opened like she was going to add something.

"I haven't heard that one before." Doctor Brown's eyebrows shot up.

"It's for Camp Moshe. Part of a new extreme sports plan." Mom summarized the details with a dutiful, straight-faced expression.

"Ahh. Good to know. We'll keep more doctors on standby." Doctor Brown winked. "I'm not sure you want any campers doing what you did, young man."

"Is it broken?"

"No, but you banged it pretty bad. I'll have to cauterize it to stop the blood flow."

His mom's lips slid into a satisfied I-told-you-so smile.

Doctor Brown clicked off his penlight. He moved to a cupboard and pulled out his supplies. "It might turn a lovely shade of purple, and if you're lucky, you won't get the accompanying black eyes. Over-the-counter pain meds should help. Ready?"

"Ready as I'll ever be."

"I'm going to use this spray to numb the area." Doctor Brown held up a container. After a couple of squirts up his nostril, he picked up a larger tool. "Now I'm going to find the exposed blood vessel and give it a little zap. This shouldn't hurt."

Kye felt an odd tickle that made him want to sneeze, and it was all over.

"That's it. Go home and ice it. Don't blow your nose for a couple of days and use petroleum jelly to keep it moist."

"Thanks, Doc." Kye slipped on the clean shirt his mother had brought him.

"Did you at least win?" Doctor Brown looked up from his clipboard.

"Win?"

"The course? I assume you were trying to win something?"

Mom laughed so hard her shoulders

heaved and threw her into a coughing fit. Did Grace tell his mom that he had been trying to get Grace's attention? Had he been that obvious?

"Not even close," Kye answered as he backed his mother away from the doctor. "Not even close."

Grace stood as they exited the exam room, concern all over her pretty face. Their gazes locked.

He grinned at her. "Like I said earlier, it's fine. We can even rock climb tomorrow."

Her expression relaxed at the word fine, then tensed again at the reminder of their rock-climbing date.

"Great," she smiled weakly.

Kye led the parade out of the hospital, struggling to get a hold of his emotions. Tomorrow's excursion was no longer about rock climbing. It was about attraction. Part of him hoped she also felt the charge that detonated every time they were together. Another part of him feared what it would mean if she did.

"Kye's accident only proves my theory." Grace stuck to her hypothesis like gum to a shoe, gritting her teeth as she helped Kate clean up the darkening beach. The setting sun shot glorious rays of color across the calm water, but Grace felt anything but calm. Why wouldn't Kate let it go?

"What theory? That a man will do anything to gain the attention of a beautiful lady?" Her prodding rubbed Grace like sandpaper. Kate had become a bit of a staff matchmaker, wanting all her co-workers as happy as she and her new fiancé. She burst with a glass-is-half-full, my grass-is-greener attitude. Kate tossed a few more empty water bottles into the recycling bin lying at her feet.

"Men don't think before they act and their haste affects everyone." Grace picked up and slammed down empty water bottles. When her dad recklessly jumped into the ocean, it changed everything. She wasn't interested in a man who spent his life taking risks, no matter how calculated.

"Come on." Kate caught Grace's hands in hers. "You don't really believe that, do you?"

Grace blinked back tears. She didn't want to explain it all to Kate. Not after reliving it earlier with Kye. "Yes, I do."

Kate stuffed her hands into her short pockets. "I think that's sad."

Grace shrugged and faced the breeze welcoming the refreshing coolness on her face. "Reckless behaviors result in injury. It's simple cause and effect."

"Life isn't always safe."

Kye had said nearly the exact thing to her. "How did I become the bad guy here? Kye was the fool who ran up the slide before checking to see if it was assembled right."

"Yeah. And when you were at the hospital, Kaleb looked over the bolts. He said they looked defective. It's lucky this happened to Kye and not one of the kids. That bolt was going to eventually break."

"Lucky? This just proves that extreme camp idea is foolish."

"Kye probably broke his nose." Kate gave her a pointed look and then scooped up the bin and headed back toward the campground.

Grace crinkled her nose and grazed it with her fingertip. Kye did have a pretty cute nose. "It's not broken," she called after Kate. She scrambled to catch up with her friend. "Why did he do that? If he's such a great catch and smart guy, what was his plan?"

"His plan was to impress you. Everybody knew it but you." Kate's ponytail bobbed with each step.

Grace stopped. Was it true? It couldn't be true. She didn't have time for romance. Besides, Kye was temporary. Off to the next business-related rescue after saving the camp. That was the plan.

She ran after Kate. "Oh, he made an impression, all right."

Kate turned.

"He left his face-print on the yellow slide." Grace's attempt at humor fell flat.

"He just wanted you to notice him. You'd ignored him all afternoon."

Oh, she noticed him all right. When Kye had hitched up his T-shirt and revealed way too much skin, she'd averted her gaze. The scrunched-up T-shirt covering half his face couldn't hide his deep dimple any better than it hid his muscular frame. Her heart had leapt. It shouldn't have, but it did.

Grace closed her eyes. *Lord, help me.*

She'd ticked off Kate tonight, and earlier Kye definitely didn't appreciate her meddling and calling his mother. She couldn't seem to get it right. But what was she supposed to do? Nothing? The guy blacks out for a few minutes and expects everyone to take it in stride? And just because Kate was getting married, Grace should follow her down the aisle with the next available guy?

"Forget it." Kate took her silence as disagreement and turned to walk away.

"Wait," Grace caught her arm and tugged her back. "I know he's a good guy. I'm just working through my own issues. OK?"

*Please, God, let it be okay.*

Kate softened. "Sure."

Grace gave her a quick hug and offered to finish cleaning up. She trudged her way back to the beach to collect the rest of the garbage. Could anything else go wrong?

"Grace?"

Grace squinted into the shadows. Her mother picked up the hem of her long skirt and jogged toward her.

Grace sighed.

"Mom, what are you doing out here?"

"Jeremy told me what happened. Is Kye OK? I know you two are friends." The faintest frown showed between her brows.

"He's going to be fine." She recalled the look on Kye's face as Tamera tugged him across the parking lot yapping about catching up on the ride back to camp. She stifled a laugh. "He'll be more than fine. Tamera is looking after him."

"Good," Ann nodded. "He's a good man."

"Yeah." Grace hid her surprise of her mother's summation of Kye's character behind a cough.

"I hear the camp's insurance adjuster is coming in a few days."

She cocked an eyebrow. Her mom never made small talk. "Yes, the day after tomorrow. How did you know?"

144

"Their receptionist is a friend of mine. She said that their office received an anonymous call expressing concern about the camp's safety."

"What?"

Ann studied Grace. "You aren't taking any unnecessary risks, are you?"

"No, Mom. We are doing everything by the book." The stolen boat, bear, net in the water, and her quick trip to the hospital with Kye flashed through her mind. But those weren't connected. And they certainly were not the camp's fault.

"OK. I just needed to ask." Mom tucked a wayward strand of hair around Grace's ear. "You're happy, right?"

Grace's eyes bugged out. "Why?"

Ann's bottom lip quivered, and she caught it between her teeth, holding it for a half second. "I've been thinking a lot lately. After you moved from the cottage to the cabin, Graham explained some things to me and . . . and, I owe you an apology." A sad smile turned up the corners of her lips. "I'm sorry, sweetheart."

The apology came so unexpectedly, Grace could only stare. "For what?"

"For not acknowledging that you are great at your job." She ran the back of her fingers down Grace's cheek and wiped away a tear.

"You know I am proud of you, right?"

Her throat tightened. "I do now."

Her mother blinked rapidly, and then pulled her shoulders back. "Good. I needed you to know that."

Ann wiped her eyes, and then laughed uncomfortably. "Well, I better get back to Jeremy before he wonders where I got off to. Good night."

"Night, Mom." Grace collected the rest of the trash and ensured it was properly stored in the bear-proof bins before returning to her cabin. She fell onto the lawn chair she'd picked up curbside and pondered her mother's apology until her phone interrupted her thoughts. Uncle Carl's voice filled her with warmth.

"Uncle Carl!"

"Gracey! I'm sorry it's taken so long to call. I've had the best vacation. Fishing is great, and the sunshine is better. But I suspect you haven't been trying to get in touch with me about my holiday. Am I right?'

She shifted on her chair. A light shone in Kye's cabin. Was he back from the hospital? Was his mother still there? "You always knew how to read in between the lines, Uncle Carl."

"How are things at camp?"

"Not what I expected."

"But Kye's working out, right? He is everything I thought he was?"

Grace hated the tension that crept into Uncle Carl's voice. He deserved this break, not to be dragged back into the drama of camp.

"I'm not thrilled with his direction, but he's a good guy." Her heart zinged as she remembered the tender way he wrapped her arm earlier in the day, and the way Kate and her mother vouched for his character.

"Is there romance blooming?" Uncle Carl's hopefulness oozed through the connection. Was that why Uncle Carl so easily stepped aside and accepted retirement? Was he matchmaking?

"We've hit some unexpected roadblocks." She ignored his question and instead briefed him on what had been happening, including her mother's bombshell of an announcement about the insurance.

"That sounds like an awful lot to process."

Her fingers ached from her grip on the phone. He didn't know the half of it. She forced her hand to relax. "We'll get through. It's not like someone is out to ruin the camp." As soon as the words left her lips, she wondered if someone could be behind all their bad luck.

"I don't know. It's too serious to be a prank, but too frequent to write off as happenstance."

"Could someone be behind this? Another camp?"

"I doubt it. They're all struggling to maintain enrollment. Most of the talk when I was there had been about working together, not against each other. Keep your wits about you."

A cold sweat beaded on her brow. What if someone was trying to sabotage the camp? What did that mean for the campers? For her program? For Kye? "Did you ever have a summer like this?"

"No," he laughed. "The worse thing I ever had to handle was an ornery board member who kept trying to buy up shares so he could gain the majority."

"What did he want with shares?"

"He said the capitol gained from selling shares would save the camp from closure, but I wasn't convinced he planned to keep the camp open. There was something fishy about the whole thing."

"He's not still here, is he?"

"Last I heard, he left the cottage to his family and moved away. I think the noise from the kids got to him."

"At least we don't have some cranky old

man to deal with on top of everything else."

"Keep me posted, Grace."

"Will do." After they disconnected, Grace remained on the porch. What would Uncle Carl think about her rock climbing plans? In light of all that had happened, would he be concerned for her safety? Should she tell Kye about her theory of sabotage?

Kye's cabin light flicked off, cloaking his place in darkness. Maybe tomorrow's excursion wasn't such a good idea.

# 9

Ignoring her ridiculous fears, Grace followed Kye up the trail leading to the largest rock formation in Camp Moshe. It didn't matter that this was the bunny slope of rock climbing, it was bigger than anything she'd ever climbed before, and that included the time she cleaned the eaves on her mother's two-story house.

"We'll start over there." Kye pointed toward the small clearing on the other side of the trail marked with a brown Camp Moshe sign nearly camouflaged by the seasonal foliage. "The anchors are in place, and I already double and triple checked them. It's solid as a rock." His lips twitched at his play on words.

Grace gulped and craned her neck back to see the peak through the tree branches obstructing her view. How bad could it be?

They walked single file through the bush toward the clearing, and she couldn't help but think she was walking the plank. "Are you sure you feel up to this?"

Kye grinned. "You heard my mom. I've had my nose cauterized *thousands* of times. It's never slowed me down before."

Great.

She swallowed the lump in her throat. If the campers could do this, so could she.

Kye kept looking back at her, his brows pulled together in concern. Did he expect her to disappear into the woods? She slashed down a wispy branch protruding at eye level. If someone was set on destroying the camp, she definitely wouldn't be safer alone in the woods. The sudden memory of Kye struggling underneath the bear sent a shudder through her body. Nope. That escape route wouldn't do for many reasons.

Kye led her into the clearing and turned to face her. He moved with steadiness and quiet assurance. Why hadn't she ever noticed how well suited he was for this lifestyle?

"Double check that your clothing doesn't restrict your movements or isn't so baggy that it can snag your equipment."

She twisted at the waist from the right to the left, stretched her arms over head, and leaned back. Then she bent forward to touch her toes. "All systems go."

He smiled. "Now, take a few deep breaths — in through the nose and out through the mouth. It'll help you relax."

She obediently let out a slow, quiet, controlled breath. It didn't work.

"I want you to stand at the bottom here," he motioned to the base of the rock in front of the first anchor. He shuffled her into place directly in front of him and leaned around her.

Heat radiated off his body. How on earth was she supposed to concentrate with him standing so close?

He pointed to the rock. "Plan your route. Adrenaline tempts even the best climber to plunge right in, but preparation is everything."

He didn't have to worry. She wasn't plunging anywhere today. She hoped.

"Figure out which bits of the climb might be hard and try to find a good rest point before them. That'll give you a chance to shake out your arms and take a breather. Then, we'll check your gear a final time and strap on a helmet."

Her insides still tap-danced from the gentle way he had tugged her into place, making it difficult to study the rock when what she really wanted was to study him. Her eyes snaked upwards, following the trail of anchors toward the peak. Had anyone tampered with them? Kye said he checked them, right?

"You made sure the anchors are safe?"

"Yup." He smiled.

She looked again. She'd likely need a break almost halfway. "Is that little ledge a good resting place?" She pointed to a small bit of rock jutting out from the side.

He grinned, seemingly pleased she had picked that spot. "It's a perfect place. We specifically chose to climb here because it offered that halfway resting point."

A surge of energy shot through her veins. She could do this. She would do this.

She squinted against the sunlight as Kye checked his equipment. In many ways, he seemed more at home here, at the base of the mountain, than he did in the office. His tanned arms moved with efficiency. She could trust him. She would trust him.

"Now let's make sure your gear is properly racked on your harness, so you can locate what you need when you need it." He tugged and pulled at the ropes and clips attached to her. She forced her mind toward the climb and away from how her stomach twisted each time he grazed her skin.

He finished by snapping the chinstrap on her helmet together. His knuckles grazed her cheek, and he paused, studying her for an uncomfortable moment. Did he question her ability to actually complete this mission? Did he regret inviting her?

She pulled back and pretended to shield her eyes from the sun, but really, she wanted to shield him from her uncertainties. How could she reassure him that she'd be fine if she wasn't convinced she could do this? That she should do this?

"Are you really OK? You don't have to do this. You have nothing to prove to me, Grace."

"I'm fine." As much as she wanted to take his offer out, for some crazy reason, she needed to prove to herself that she could conquer her fears and anything else life sent her way.

He nodded. "Remember, don't overuse your arms. That's a rookie mistake. As you climb higher, clip your belay rope onto the anchors in the rock. That will prevent you from falling too far should you lose your footing."

Her gut heaved at the word fall. She briefly pinched her eyes shut.

"Push with your legs and conserve your energy using mostly the big toe."

"Why the big toe?"

"It's more sensitive, it gives you better

awareness of your grip."

She inhaled hard. "OK. I'm as ready as I'll ever be."

"Remember to keep your eyes on the rock in front of you and slightly above. Don't look down. The bolts are in place. You go ahead, and I'll follow." He snapped on his own helmet and picked up the belay, locking off the rope.

Knowing Kye held her rope eased the invisible fist squeezing her chest. She stepped close to the rock face and grazed her fingers over the surface. It was cooler than she expected. She hooked onto her first anchor and wiggled her toes, which now felt incredibly cramped inside her shoes and dipped her fingers inside the chalk bag. She dragged them through, turning them white and powdery. No more delays.

Kye watched her with an amused expression, completely attuned to her stalling methods.

She took a deep breath and grabbed the rock, placed her right foot on the first hold and pushed up, remembering Kye's instruction to use her legs.

"Climbing," she said, as she had been instructed to do.

"Climb on," he replied pulling out some rope.

Maybe it wouldn't be as tough as she had anticipated? She literally put her life in his hands and struggled through the first move. She resisted the urge to look down at Kye as she moved higher and higher. A strong desire to see his approval coursed through her body, but she needed to look up, not down. She forced herself upward.

She felt for her next hold, and a loose piece of rock gave way. She cried out before she could stop herself. Then she clamped her mouth shut, tightened her core, and pulled herself in close to the wall. *Please, God, help me do this. Keep me safe.*

Was it fair of her to ask God to keep her safe when she willingly went into this dangerous situation? Was that as naïve as choosing to sin and planning to ask for forgiveness later?

She drew a deep breath. This wasn't the time for deep theological thoughts. She clipped her rope onto the next anchor. It sagged too much.

"Up rope!" Her arms burned as she waited for Kye to pull the slack out of the rope. Nothing. Couldn't he hear her? She chanced a glance down. The rope had snagged on a rock projecting from the surface. Kye yanked on it to tighten it, but no luck.

"It's stuck," he called.

Great. She sucked in another breath. Lord, Kye's mother was right. This was stupid. Her fingers and arms had lost the tingle of excitement and had long ago gone numb. Could she get to her resting spot before they gave out? Should she go back to the last place she felt safe and relax her arms? She scrambled to remember what Kye told her to do.

Everything felt wrong.

A rustling above dragged her gaze up. A shadow loomed over the edge. Was someone there? A fumbling in the loose shale rang through the quiet.

"Rock!" Kye screamed. "Take!"

She didn't question him. She pushed herself off the wall and surrendered to gravity. Her rope snapped taut, jolting her body. She swung away from all that was safe, and a shower of rocks scraped the skin from her left arm. Suspended by her harness, a scream tore from her throat.

She clawed for the rocky surface, desperate to find a hold strong enough to support her weight. Rocks and dirt cut into her hands as small pebbles cascaded like a waterfall.

She looked down.

The stones fell and fell, raining around Kye, who held her rope with a look in his eyes that shot fear through her body.

Kye sprinted backwards to take up the rope's slack. *Lord, help me.* Rocks and stones ricocheted off his helmet. Why had he goaded her into climbing?

Her scream shredded his heart. She clamored for a hold, and sediment and debris rained down, peeling her tender arm raw. This was his fault. His fault.

"I've got you, Grace! Hang on!" His foot slipped in the loose soil. He leaned back to better support her full weight on the rope and fought the pull, keeping the rope at a forty-five-degree angle. *Lord, help!*

The line burned through his thin gloves. But he would die before he let her fall.

They locked eyes. The terror etched on her face cut deep. He did this. Caused this. He had to fix it. He had to get her out from under the falling stones.

Before he could direct her, she pulled herself together with admirable grit, found a safe hold and stabilized, easing the tension on the rope.

The shower of gravel and stones subsided.

He held fast, moving to the left of her, slowly giving her just enough rope to maneuver.

*Thank you!*

He manipulated the rope, tightening the slack. "That's right, Grace. To your right is your resting place. Can you make it there?"

"I think so." Her muscles had to be screaming in protest by now. How was she doing this?

He let out a bit more rope.

Her trembling hand reached out and gingerly tested another hold before she trusted her weight to it. She jockeyed herself sideways until she finally sat on the small ledge.

He immediately tightened the slack, locked the rope, and breathed.

She leaned back against the rock face, eyes closed, lips moving, praying. He'd never seen such a beautiful sight.

He wanted to drop in a "thanks, Lord" too, but he didn't dare let his guard down. Not until she was completely safe. And that meant getting her off the side of this rock.

Even from the ground he could see the dampness trailing down her white cheeks. But it was the resolve in her eyes that somersaulted through his insides. This girl was a fighter. How was it possible he ever saw her any other way?

"When you're ready, you'll lean back onto the rope, and I'll lower you down," he called.

"No." She didn't budge off the wall.

"You can do this, Grace. I know you can."

"No." She shot him an indecipherable look through narrowed eyes. Chest heaving, she folded her arms and winced in pain.

Determined or stubborn?

"The harness will hold you. You can't stay on the ledge forever."

She snapped her eyes fully open, and her gaze landed on him with more weight than the falling stones that had hit his helmet. "I don't plan to stay here. I'm reaching the top."

She carefully stood and brushed the dust off her hands, unable to hide the way her knees knocked despite her obvious determination to look unafraid. Her killer stare challenged him to deny her the right to conquer the climb.

He quickly adjusted the rope to accommodate her standing position. "Are you sure?"

"As sure as I've ever been."

"What about your arm?" The raw skin scraped pink would make climbing the rest of the way even more difficult than before.

"I can do it," she asserted. A stubborn expression flashed across her face. She grabbed a hold, glanced his way, brandished a wobbly grin, and shouted, "Climbing!"

He grinned back, adjusting the rope. "Climb on."

He talked her through the rest of the climb, and within thirty minutes, they rested together on top of the rocky formation they named Yahweh-Yireh, meaning the Lord will provide. He treated her wound with the first aid supplies he'd packed, joking that their camp nurse would have her work cut out for herself just tending to the two of them.

They sat down, and Grace leaned back against him. They looked down over Lake Moshe and the distant campground. For the first time since meeting Grace, he questioned his judgment and second-guessed his plans for Camp Moshe. Was a sport camp too dangerous? Was *he* too reckless?

A contented sigh slipped out of Grace. "You know, when you first mentioned rock climbing as an elective, I thought you were crazy."

"I know." Maybe he was crazy. Maybe this whole idea was crazy. Maybe she was right all along.

"Then I wondered where on earth would you find a mountain? Most of the rock formations around here have a hikeable, gentle incline."

"You don't need a lot of height to practice rock climbing. These rock formations are perfect for starters. Further up Klymer trail are some great places. Caves, crevices, and cliffs."

She nudged him. "After climbing up the cliff face of this rock, I'd have to agree. Camp Moshe's rocks provide all the excitement you need."

Pride in her decision to complete the climb filled him to bursting. "You climbed the hardest one. We have smaller ones marked out for the younger kids. You were amazing, you know." He tipped his head forward and spoke the words into her hair. "I can't believe you finished after that scare."

She shrugged. "I knew if I didn't, I'd never come back out again. And even I have to admit, as scary as that was, sitting here on the top, looking down and seeing where I've come from, feels pretty great. I get the addiction, the thrill."

He shaded his eyes. "Do you see that?"

A hooded man hiked down the path below them.

"Who is it?"

"I don't know. Could be Kaleb or Eric checking the anchors for the kids. Could be anybody."

She shuddered.

He wrapped his arms around her, pulling her closer.

"Right before that rock came down, I thought I saw a shadow. I assumed it was an animal but —"

"You think somebody was up there?" Kye jumped to his feet and scoured the path. There was no sight of the hooded man.

He sank back down.

Grace filled in Kye on her chat with Uncle Carl and her theories.

Had his letter writer escalated to actual physical danger? "I've received a few threats —"

"Threats?" Grace's body went rigid.

"Nothing I've never dealt with before while revamping a company." He loved how she leaned into him as if closer contact between them made her feel safe. "I haven't received a new letter since before the bear, so I assumed the threat was gone." Except Ron had expressed the possibility the bear had been intentionally lured. "Typically, once people see that the changes I make are working, the opposition dies off." Kye rubbed his hands through his hair.

"But this can't all be bad luck. What are the chances those bolts from that slide arrived rusty? Or that netting *just happened* to find its way into the water?"

"Kaleb and Eric's dad is trying to buy the land," Kye ignored her questions, not liking where they led. "But they wouldn't endanger the campers, would they? Or purposefully hurt you?"

She shrugged. "Kaleb did help Bobby put the defective slide together."

Kye pulled her in close. "Impossible. Kaleb wouldn't hurt you on purpose. There must be another explanation." It felt right to tuck her warm and strong body close to his. A gentle breeze sent wisps of her hair across his face. He inhaled vanilla, and wondered briefly if she tasted like vanilla too.

"I'll look into Kaleb and see if anything seems suspicious. I won't let anything happen to you or our campers." He didn't really think Kaleb — or anyone else for that matter — was behind this. In the past, this sort of thing had always turned out to be nothing. But he didn't like her looking so scared.

She twisted and looked into his eyes. Did she question his sincerity? Her face, mere inches away, stole his planned words. Hot breath charged the air between them.

Her lips, all moist and soft, curved into a smile. If he leaned in the tiniest bit, their mouths would meet, and he would finally know if she tasted like vanilla too. His lips tingled and his breath shortened. He studied her face, looking for permission.

Her eyes slid shut.

He wrestled with desire. He was her boss, not her boyfriend. Would it be fair to act on his growing feelings for her when his next job would move him away far too soon? He hardened himself and obeyed his conscience. He bypassed her lips and pressed his mouth to her forehead.

Her eyes fluttered open, revealing disappointment. She pulled away, but he tightened his arms and tugged her back, feathering his breath across her ear. "Don't."

"Don't what?" she whispered.

"Don't go."

She studied him for a second longer and then relaxed into his embrace.

He tenderly stroked up and down her injured arm and impulsive words spilled out. "You know, you're not the person I first thought you were."

She tipped her head back. Her smile reached her eyes and lit them. "Neither are you, Kye Campton. Neither are you."

# 10

"As you can see, we've spared no expense in choosing the best and safest equipment for the camp. The wellbeing of our campers is of utmost concern." Kye wiped his damp palms on his jeans. The insurance adjuster had insisted on visiting the camp in person when usually sending in the brochures and activity details were enough to determine a premium. It had to be connected to that anonymous tip Grace told him about.

Tony adjusted his folder in his hands and flipped through papers. "Yes, we have the details of your equipment here." Tony looked like he'd rather be anywhere than here swatting horse flies.

"What happened there?" Tony pointed to the exterior of the dining hall scheduled for repair later this week.

Kye stifled a groan. Why didn't he fix it sooner?

"Everything else is so well maintained . . ."

Tony's voice trailed off leaving Kye to fill in his blanks.

"I'll complete those repairs before the campers arrive." Kye avoided the question. Tony needed to conclude that extreme sports didn't equate to extreme risk and a dining hall signed by a bear's claws wouldn't help his case.

Tony scribbled more notes, paused, looked up, and then wrote some more, never once making eye contact with Kye. "I was here," Tony shuffled through his notes, "less than a year ago. I don't remember that damage. What happened?"

Kye jammed his hands into his front jean pockets. "We had an issue with a black bear, but the Ministry of Natural Resources sent out a guy who collared and relocated him."

Tony finally looked at him. "That's right. I saw that on the news."

So he already knew about the bear. Was Tony trying to test his integrity with a trick question?

"Bears are normal for all the campgrounds around here," Tony said. He made another note. "It would only become an issue if you were negligent in some way." Tony peered over the top of his clipboard and drilled his gaze into Kye.

Kye fought the urge to squirm like a

reprimanded schoolboy. Did Tony know? *Lord, please bless my honesty.* "We did leave some food out one night after a staff picnic, which might have attracted the animal." Kye held Tony's stare. Since they had no proof, he didn't add Ron's suspicions that someone purposefully baited the bear. "But it's all taken care of now."

The adjuster made another silent note and stepped closer to inspect the dining hall's back door where the worst of the exterior damage remained.

Kye wanted to kick himself. He could have had this fixed already if he hadn't been so distracted with Grace.

"That's a lot of damage for one bear."

"Yes, it is. But it was only one bear. We've had no other sightings since he's been relocated." Kye clamped his mouth shut. This wasn't the time to start babbling. Sweat drizzled down his back. What he had hoped was a cursory visit from their insurance provider suddenly felt like much more.

Laughter trickled up from the lake. Grace and Jeremy splashed around in the gentle waves as they returned to the beach.

"I thought your campers weren't arriving for two more days?"

"Jeremy is a local boy, and that's his sister."

"But the girl, she's wearing a Camp Moshe shirt, right?" Tony watched Grace a little too intently for Kye's liking.

"Yes, she's an instructor this summer."

"A life guard?"

"Not exactly. She's running a pilot program called Water Survival for Non-Swimmers. If it does well, the government will fund her to take it province-wide. We sent you the brochure."

Tony rooted around for the brochure Grace designed and tugged it out. He flipped it over and looked at the back, clipping it onto his board. "Non-swimmers in the water? They wear life vests, I assume?" Tony made a few more notes, glancing up frequently to study Grace.

What on earth was he writing? A novel?

"Ah, it might be better if she explains the program." Kye led Tony toward Grace. Glistening water droplets in Grace's hair reflected the sunlight, and the tender smile she sent his way made Kye's stomach flip.

She pulled her hair over one tanned shoulder and wrung out the water. "Hi, Kye."

"Hi." Kye ruffled Jeremy's hair. "How was your swim?"

"Great!" Jeremy piped up. "Grace is going to teach me how to stay afloat in rough water. I can't wait!"

Why couldn't she teach him beach volleyball or something equally benign today? "That's great."

Tony cleared his throat.

"Grace, this is Tony, a representative from our insurance company. He'd like to know more about your program. He's here to make the final quote for our camp insurance."

Grace studied Tony for a half beat, as if she were trying to get a read on the situation. Then she flashed her best saleswoman smile. "I'd love to tell you all about my program. I had the stable hand tack a horse for me, and I'd hate to change my mind about riding. It's bad barn etiquette. If you let me see Jeremy home, you can walk with me to the stables. Maybe that'll be enough time to cover your questions."

Tony straightened up and smiled for the first time since arriving. "I'll wait here. Take your time, sweetheart."

Kye bristled at the unprofessional endearment. Sure, some older men called every young woman *dear* or *sweetheart,* and it meant nothing. But the way Tony flashed his pearly whites made Kye's stomach heave.

Grace paused a half second, flicked her

gaze from Tony's eager expression to Kye, and then ushered Jeremy home. In a short time, she returned dressed in a casual, loose-fitting T-shirt and jeans. She fell into step beside Tony.

"So tell me more about your program."

Grace chatted up a storm. Kye followed a half step behind, praying the whole way. He didn't need to stay, but he wasn't about to leave Grace with Tony after that weird sweetheart comment.

Why wasn't Tony taking notes now? He seemed more intrigued by the beautiful way Grace accentuated her words with hand gestures. He resisted the urge to nudge Grace into a faster walking pace.

"I am basically taking non-swimmers and teaching them what to do in the event they fall into deep water. The first step is flip, float, and scream. The second step is to teach them to tread water for one minute and swim fifty meters."

"Is it risky?" Tony leaned in a bit closer than needed. An uncharacteristic urge shot through Kye to wedge himself between the two of them.

Grace moved back, and redirected his attention to her program by pointing at her brochure clipped to his clipboard. "All the details are in there. It's no more risky than traditional swimming lessons. Everyone is a non-swimmer until they learn."

Tony nodded and glanced at the stables looming ahead as if he was annoyed they were reaching them so quickly. He shortened his stride.

"Water Survival for Non-Swimmers is a perfect summer camp program because lakes and rivers are the settings that account for more than half of the drownings of children aged five to twelve," Grace continued. "And two-thirds of those drownings happen while the children are playing in the water."

Kye groaned. Throwing stats at a numbers guy was worse than outright flirting. She was speaking his language. Tony's eyes lit up.

Awareness crept into Grace's expression. Her smile strained, and her usually fluid movements became jerky. She reached back for Kye and tugged him closer to her. "I'm sure Kye can provide you with any additional information you need."

Slam!

Tony blinked and then scribbled some notes. His incessant note-taking had been driving Kye crazy earlier, but he welcomed it now. Anything to get this guy's attention off of Grace.

Tony removed his glasses, folded them, and tucked them into his upper breast pocket. "Sounds a little risky considering those numbers."

Would he let Grace's polite rejection affect his decision? Tony had to see the value in this kind of program because if they couldn't get insurance, they couldn't open the camp.

"It's not risky, not really." Grace's smile relaxed when Kye placed his hand at the small of her back. "From those numbers, three quarters of them were either alone, non-swimmers, or without adult supervision. Part of Water Survival for Non-Swimmers is to teach preventative measures — teach the kids to make wiser decisions and report to a lifeguard when they see peers making foolish choices."

"Hmm." Tony jotted notes like a clerical pro.

Grace's eyes flashed. She didn't take kindly to anyone questioning the validity of her program. On any other day, Kye might enjoy the fireworks, but he needed Tony to leave convinced that Camp Moshe was a safe place for kids.

"What happened to your arm?" Tony pointed his pen to the healing scrapes on the side of Grace's arm.

She glanced down to the scabs. "Nothing serious. Minor rock climbing mishap." As soon as the words left her lips, Kye wished he could have bleeped them out.

"Rock climbing?" Tony flipped through his folder and pulled out another brochure featuring a boy climbing up the side of a rock face.

"It was no big deal," Grace rushed on to explain.

"Looks like it hurt."

Kye stiffened.

"Did the equipment malfunction?"

"No, nothing like that!" Grace exclaimed. "Some loose rock tumbled over the edge. It grazed me on the way down."

Kye didn't think this adjustment could get any worse. What were the odds that the rejected middle-aged insurance adjuster would come through for them? It would take a miracle to get them insured now.

Tony smiled an eerie, unreadable smile, his gaze moving from where Grace's hand rested on Kye's arm, to Kye's stiff stance. "I think I understand. That'll be all, thank you, Miss Stone."

Grace lifted her white face and looked at Kye.

"Go ahead," he nudged her. "If you're going to have any time to ride, you need to go now."

Grace hurried into the barn, and Tony's beady eyes followed her.

Kye hoped Grace enjoyed the ride. It might be her last opportunity if Tony pulled their insurance.

Why didn't she keep her big mouth shut? Instead, thoughtless words had surged from her lips like a tsunami. Again.

"Lord, when am I going to learn?" She stomped toward the barn. "I exasperated the bear. I got hurt saving Bisket. Rocks fall on me. No one is out to sabotage this camp. I'm the liability." She kicked a stick from her path.

The best way for her to help was to stay out of sight and let Kye work his business magic and seal the deal. That's why he'd nudged her toward the barn. To get her out of the way.

Why did she always get in the way?

She slammed face-first into Shawn, the stable hand.

"Whoo, what's got you so worked up?" He placed his hands on her shoulder and pushed her back from his chest.

Heat rushed to her face. Did he hear her angry self-talk?

"Sorry," she stammered. She dragged her booted foot across the dirt floor. "Is Sweet Breeze ready?"

Shawn took his time answering. She lifted her downcast eyes and caught his slow gaze trailing up and then down her frame. She didn't feel assaulted like she did when the insurance guy had so obviously appraised her, but she still folded her arms over her chest. She shuffled toward a darkened corner so the appraiser's prying eyes wouldn't witness whatever Shawn had to say.

When Shawn caught her gaze, the look in his eyes held no apology for his scrutiny. "The horse is ready. You just have to tighten the cinch."

"Thanks," she moved to brush past him, but he caught her arm. "Are you OK? Are you sure you want to ride like this?"

She shook off his hand. "I'm a capable rider. You know that."

He interrupted with a negative shake of his head. "It's my job to take care of these beauties, and your focus isn't on riding when you're all riled up. I suggest you deal with whatever or whoever has ticked you off. The horse will be ready when you are."

She bit back a retort. She had ticked herself off. How was she supposed to deal

176

with that? She counted backwards from five, let out a controlled breath, and then forced a smile.

"Thanks, Shawn. I'll take a minute before mounting."

He stepped aside and let her pass.

She resisted the urge to turn around and see if he still watched her. Her breath ingested the molasses from the sweet feed, combined with the pleasant scent of leather. The animals exhaled a symphony of sounds as the outside breeze gently rocked the rustic structure of the barn. Maybe she should apply to be a stable hand. Hidden behind walls. Unobservable to the general population.

The stall door creaked open. Shafts of light pierced the rough-hewn wood that made the barn walls. Sweet Breeze stamped his feet to ward off the relentless flies. He lifted his head as she entered.

Grace dug into her pocket and offered the chestnut a sugar cube. She scratched him between the eyes and then settled her hand on his neck. His skin and muscles twitched and quivered under her tentative touch. She nuzzled his neck, inhaling his earthiness. No animal deserved the brunt end of her frustration. She ran her hand down his velvety, short hair, feeling the steel of his muscles.

She calmed.

Lifting each hoof one at a time, Grace checked for stones. As she moved through the motions of preparing to ride, she caught a glimpse of Kye and Tony through the slats in the wood. What was taking the guy so long to leave? Their tack was sound. The horses vet checked. Kye even had shiny new latches put on the stall doors after Sweet Breeze figured out how to open the latch.

She shifted and positioned the horse between her and the spaced boards to ensure they couldn't see her.

Out of sight. Out of mind.

Hopefully.

Her insides clenched like she was coming up from a deep-water dive.

She completed her tasks, but her thoughts stayed with Kye. Was Tony still going on about her *dangerous* program? Or had Kye managed to steer the conversation onto safer topics? Fighting the urge to peek through the crack to see if they'd left the stables, she stayed close to Sweet Breeze.

Footsteps crunched. *No! Please, God, not them!*

Shawn walked by and paused at the gate. He gave her the once over.

She forced a wide smile. He could size

her up all he wanted. She was riding this horse as soon as the men left, and she'd stay out until Tony had packed up for the day. No way was she getting caught in the middle of his adjustment again.

Shawn tipped the brim of his hat, seemingly satisfied with whatever he saw.

Good.

She peeked through the slats. Nothing stirred. It was safe.

Her breath rushed out in a whoosh.

She unlooped the reins and led the horse out of the stall. She checked the cinch, and without bothering to wait for Shawn, she mounted up and gently squeezed her lower legs to cue the horse to walk. They trotted out, just as Tony and Kye rounded the corner of the barn.

Her gut clenched. Tony leaned against the fence as if settling in to watch her ride. What now? She couldn't exactly turn the horse around and go back into the barn. She gave Sweet Breeze a gentle kick. He geared into a canter.

Why didn't she wait a few more minutes before coming out?

Grace leaned forward. Her helmet prevented the wind from whipping through her hair, but her ponytail still slapped metrically against her back. The gentle and rhythmic rocking of Sweet Breeze under her body slowed her mind.

*God, will you fix this mess?*

She drew strength from the contact between her body and the horse. His rippling muscles contracted against her calves. Her heels pushed down, stretching her calves and putting pressure on her foot. For a minute, everything slipped away but the pleasure of riding.

Then, it all shifted. Sweet Breeze threw his weight into his shoulder. The saddle slipped. She tightened her calves but couldn't hold her seat. *No!* She dangled dangerously close to the fence, each board whipping past her face.

"Whoa! Whoa!" She clung to the horse.

Sweet Breeze stopped.

Grace slid off the side of Sweet Breeze, the momentum pitching her into the rough wood. Pain shot through her shoulder, and she crumpled to the ground.

Roaring dimmed.

The fuzz cleared.

She blinked.

She wiggled a leg. Then another. Each arm. Then tentatively moved her head. *Thank you, God, that I was wearing a helmet!*

Kye's hands turned her over, and his

widened eyes roamed her body. "Are you OK?"

"Oh!" She groaned. "This is gonna hurt tomorrow." She pushed away Kye's hands and eyed Shawn, who arrived a half-beat behind Kye. "I'm fine." She stood. She eyed Sweet Breeze, grazing nearby as if nothing out of the ordinary had occurred.

Shawn stepped between her and the horse, forcing her to focus on him. "I told you to tighten the cinch. Didn't you check it?"

Grace paused. Did she? She'd checked the hooves. She'd given him a sugar cube. She'd grabbed her helmet. She'd checked the cinch. She must have. A good rider always double-checked the cinch. Always.

"I . . . I . . . I don't remember." She bounced her gaze from Shawn to Kye, who still hovered closer than necessary, and then back to Shawn. "I meant to but —" She glanced at Kye.

"You got distracted." Shawn finished for her. His pulled-in brows and frown sent shame coursing through her body. She knew better.

"You could have been seriously hurt," Kye whispered.

She knew it. If the pain in her thigh was any indication, she was going to have a killer bruise there, but if that was all that surfaced, then she'd gotten off lucky.

She glanced past Kye to Tony, who stood at the fence furiously taking notes.

So much for staying out of sight. The tsunami was coming.

# 11

Kye's computer mouse hovered over the unread e-mail that displayed Tony's contact information in bold font. Tony. The man Grace shot down. The man warned about the camp by some disgruntled member of the community. The man with the ability to bring his revitalization plan to a screeching halt.

He pulled open his top desk drawer and removed a package of fennel seeds. His mother had pressed them into his hands when they'd left the hospital together after his up-close-and-personal look at their new obstacle course. She'd assured him that chewing the seeds would relieve his cramping and nausea and miraculously heal his ulcer. She couldn't seem to get it through her head that ulcers were treated with antibiotics. He popped a few in his mouth and chomped away at the bird food.

They didn't work. His stomach churned.

He stared at the computer screen.

*Please, God, let us get this insurance.* For a crazy minute, he didn't want to open the e-mail and entertain the possibility that he'd failed in his assignment. *Please, God.* He reached for the mouse.

Grace popped her head in the room. "Busy?"

He yanked his hands off the keys and closed his laptop. She didn't need to worry about the insurance. That was his job.

"What's up?"

Before she could speak, Judy paused at the door and smiled at them. "Can I get either of you a coffee?"

Grace's features tightened. "No, thanks." Kye caught Grace's gaze, and she dropped it to the floor.

He shrugged in response to Judy's perplexed expression. "We're fine. Thanks, Judy." He motioned for her to move on.

The minute Judy rounded the corner, Grace pulled her phone out of her pocket and strode into the room. She silently punched her index finger against her phone screen as she rapidly closed the distance between them.

He cocked his head. "Care to tell me what this is all about?"

"Look at this." She thrust her phone

under Kye's nose and thumbed through some pictures. Saddle after saddle after saddle. Did she want him to buy more equipment for the stables?

His brow tightened. "What am I looking at?"

"The cinch, Kye. This is the saddle Shawn had on Sweet Breeze yesterday. Look at the cinch." She thrust the phone forward. If she'd rammed it any closer to his face, she would've punched him in the nose. He briefly wrapped his hands around her trembling ones before taking the cell from her. Something had her worked up.

He flipped through the images. He still didn't get it. "I'm sorry, but I'm not sure what I am looking for here." He handed the device back to her.

She let out an exasperated sigh. "Come with me." She grabbed his hand and hauled him from behind his desk.

"Where are we going?" He shook loose, snatched his phone off the desk, and clipped it to his belt.

"The stables."

Her powerful angry steps forced Kye to jog to catch up. He caught up with her outside the building. She slowed just enough to enable them to converse but stayed a half step ahead.

"Fill me in," he panted.

"Someone tampered with the cinch on my saddle. That's why I fell. Someone rigged it to fail."

"Are you sure?" A surge of nausea rolled through him as an image of Grace crumpled by the fence flashed though his mind. The few seconds it took to reach her side had stretched forever.

"I'll show you." Grace briefly paused at the double doors leading into the barn, looking for staff. When they found none, some of the tension left her frame. She navigated through the empty stable.

They reached the tack room where old cast iron saddle racks sat below a line of bridle hooks. The lingering scent of saddle soap with beeswax enveloped them as Grace pulled down the string cinch still attached to one side of the western saddle. She pointed to multiple broken strings and then fanned out the frayed edges across her palm.

Kye took it from her. "Can that just be wear and tear?"

She shook her head. "No. Shawn would replace a strap like this. It's compromised." A visible shudder travelled through her body.

Kye tensed. "Unless Shawn's involved." A horse stamped its feet in a nearby stall, and the thin barn walls groaned. A rustling sound from a shadowed corner raised the hairs on his neck.

Grace paced. "I knew I tightened the cinch. I knew it."

He peered into the shaded corner. Was someone there or was her sabotage theory messing with his head? He stepped in front of Grace and faced the darkness.

A cat jumped out with a screech and scurried out of the building.

He sagged. Her conspiracy talk was making him paranoid. "How could Shawn miss this? How did you miss it?"

"Because of where it is. I couldn't see the weak spot. But whoever tacked up the horse should have seen it."

"That leaves Shawn."

"Need something, boss?" Shawn sauntered in from the doors that opened onto the fenced arena where they trained new horses. How long had he been there?

"Who tacked up Sweet Breeze for Grace yesterday?"

Grace tensed, clenching and releasing her jaw.

Kye placed his hand on the small of her back. Nothing would happen to her here. Not if he could help it.

Shawn gripped the back of his neck with

his hand and looked up to the ceiling as if trying to remember. "I'm not sure. When I took my lunch break, I left the stable staff with a list of jobs. Why?"

"You were the only one here when I came to ride." Grace interjected.

"I sent them on break when I returned. What's this about?"

Kye held up his hand to stop Grace from answering. "We're not sure yet. I'm going to need to take this cinch back to the office."

Shawn's eyebrows lifted, but he didn't question him. "Sure thing." He removed it from the saddle and handed it to Kye.

Kye leveled a look at Grace, hoping she would understand the need for secrecy.

She nodded.

Kye motioned for Grace to lead the way out of the stable, and he followed her out. Halfway to the office, his phone vibrated. "Hold up, Grace." He stopped to thumb through his messages.

Kye couldn't imagine Shawn pulling a stunt like this. But who else had access? And what on earth would motivate someone to hurt Grace? Surely not Kaleb. His dad couldn't be that desperate for the camp property.

He forced his tightening neck muscles to stretch by tipping his head to the side.

Escalation from vandalism to physical threats meant it was time to notify the authorities, especially since their campers arrived tomorrow.

"What if —"

Kye held up his hand. "We don't know if this is a safe place to talk."

Grace's eyes widened.

"We'll meet tonight after work. Seven? We'll get dinner and make a list of everyone we can think of who might profit from ruining Camp Moshe."

He hated the way her tanned complexion paled. If he had taken her suspicions seriously after the rock climbing accident maybe this wouldn't have happened. No way was he second-guessing her again. The cinch proved someone was stirring the waters. But why?

Another e-mail came in. This one from the twins' dad. Probably another offer to purchase.

How convenient. If Tony's unread message said their insurance was yanked, at least he'd have an offer to present to the board. His thumb wavered over Tony's message. Without insurance, there'd be no Camp Moshe and the camp wouldn't fail because of a saboteur, it would fail because of him and his inability to pull it together.

He pursed his lips and opened the message.

"Yes!" Kye punched the air.

"What's going on?" Grace pulled her eyebrows together.

He read the email again. Slower. Their insurance premium had increased, which Kye expected due to the nature of the camp, but the message didn't contain the new payment schedule. The new payment schedule would come in a separate e-mail.

"We got camp insurance!"

A grin split her face. "It's about time we had some good news."

He resisted the urge to frown. He didn't want to cramp her happiness, but what were the odds the insurance increase would be minimal?

His stomach knotted, and he did some fast math. They had limited wiggle room. He'd spent most of the budget on the new camp equipment. The increase needed to be small for the camp to survive.

Grace nudged Kye with her shoulder, still smiling.

He grinned. No use in borrowing trouble. Today had enough.

Kye went to lock his phone screen so he could clip it back on his belt when an e-mail transitioned from unread to read status, but

Kye hadn't opened it. "Wait . . ."

Grace paused.

He swiped at the screen. More unread e-mails transitioned to read status. "No, no, no, no!" He took off running toward his office. Someone was on his computer.

"Kye!" Grace yelled after him. He heard her pounding feet behind.

He careened around the corner of the office building and sprinted through the doors. Judy half-stood from her chair as he rushed by and tossed the cinch at her desk.

He burst into his office and slammed the door against the wall.

No one.

A drop of sweat rolled down his temple. Impossible.

He circled his desk, pulled out his chair, and looked underneath.

Empty.

His fisted hands relaxed.

Grace sprinted in and pulled up short, breathing hard. "What's going on?"

"Someone gained access to my computer and read my e-mails." Kye sat down and pulled his chair up to his desk. He scrolled through his inbox. Was anything else compromised?

"How is that possible?" Grace sank into the chair across from him.

"They must have remotely hacked in."

Judy hovered in the doorway. "Everything OK?"

"Was anyone in my office today?"

"No. No one came in."

"Thanks, Judy." He dismissed her. "Please close the door."

Grace waited until the door clicked before speaking. "Why would someone hack your computer?"

"I don't know." Was it just for the e-mail? How long has it been happening? What if they had sent out messages posing as him?

Kye opened his sent folder and reviewed his outgoing messages. Nothing out of the ordinary. Unless they had sent something and then deleted it.

"What are you going to do?"

"Cut them off." He immediately shut down all external interfaces on the network, disconnecting everything from the outside world. That would stop the active attack. He then followed the steps he'd learned in the mandatory hacking class he took last fall. He logged onto the security page and changed his settings and password. That should keep the imposter out. At least for now.

Grace looked over the administration desk

that stretched the length of the lobby. Where did the cinch go? "You tossed it here, Kye. Right?"

"Yes." Kye moved behind the chest-high counter.

"I saw it land here." Grace pointed near the middle of the counter for the officer taking their statement. "I was only a few steps behind him."

They had filled in Officer Ryley on all the events leading up to their discovery of the tampered cinch, but the cinch was their only tangible proof that their story wasn't some crazy conspiracy theory.

"Maybe it fell behind?" Ryley suggested, but he didn't look hopeful they'd retrieve anything.

Kye opened and closed a few cupboards. "Judy?"

Judy stepped forward, wringing her hands. "I remember you tossed something on the desk." Her eyes darted from the officer to Kye and back to the officer. "But I'm not sure what a cinch is. And when you raced through here, I followed you into the office to see what was wrong. When I came out, there was nothing on the desk. I honestly didn't think about it until now."

Ryley jotted some notes on his pad then settled his intense stare on Judy, which seemed to unravel her even more. "Was anyone else in the lobby when Kye and Grace returned?"

"No one, sir," her voice wobbled.

Because she was involved or unnerved? Grace sagged against the desk. Without the cinch, they had no proof that the saddle had been tampered with.

Ryley's eyes softened as he turned back to Grace. "Can anyone else support your statement? Stable staff?"

Grace inwardly groaned. Kye didn't let her tell Shawn what had happened. "No, sir. We are the only ones that saw the cinch."

He flipped his notepad shut. "I don't see why you'd have any reason to lie, so I suspect something fishy is underway, but without any evidence, there is nothing I can do. I suggest you keep your wits about you and proceed with caution." He handed Grace his card. "The more serious incidents seem to be centered on you. Any chance this is personal?"

Grace froze. Personal? Could this be about her and have nothing to do with the camp? "I . . . I don't know . . ."

Kye's hand pressed against her back. When did he move to her side?

Ryley looked from Grace to Kye and then back to Grace. "Call me if anything else comes up."

Kye shook the officer's hand. "Will do. Thanks for coming."

Thanks for coming? A lot of good that did. Kye wasn't the one tossed from the horse or caught in a rainstorm of rocks. She didn't understand at all. What must they endure for the law to take them seriously? An injury? A death?

Later that evening, she glanced at the clock hanging on the wall of her room. She had less than ten minutes before Kye arrived. She bit her lip and considered the sundress in her hands. How should a woman dress for a dinner that may or may not be a date? She shoved the dress back into the closet. Not in a dress like that.

She settled on a pink, flimsy, sheer blouse combined with a matching camisole and dark jeans. A casual pair of wedge shoes and nude shoulder bag would keep it simple. Like she wasn't trying too hard.

She blew a stray strand of hair out of her eyes. Who was she kidding? She was trying really hard to look like she didn't care. But she did. She cared very much.

She pulled a brush through her hair and left it in soft waves around her shoulders. A dab of lip gloss completed the look. She glanced at her watch. Two minutes to spare.

Kye's crunchy footsteps carried through the cabin screen window. The window framed him perfectly as he made his way across the trail connecting their cabins. When the porch groaned under his weight, she swung open the door.

His eyes widened. "You look amazing!"

She hid her pleasure. "Thank you." She grabbed her purse and pulled the door closed behind her. "Is your mother joining us tonight?" Her lips twitched as a blush flushed his features at the reference to their last dinner out.

He grinned. "No mothers tonight. And to ensure it" — he made a show of pulling out his phone and putting it on silent — "everything is off."

Her stomach fluttered and made it hard to catch her breath. She placed a hand on her midriff and reminded herself why he was all wrong for her. He was leaving soon. He was transient. Her program needed to come first. Unfortunately, one look into his eyes made her forget all reason.

*It's not a date.*

Gentle pressure on the small of her back guided her toward his vehicle.

"I made a reservation at a little place a few miles up the lake. It's small, but the food is excellent. All local produce and a seasonal menu. I think you'll like it."

They chit-chatted until they arrived and were seated on the outside patio adjacent to the lake. The waiter lit a candle inside a small crystal dish. The flame generated an ambiance of romance, and Grace's cheeks heated. *It's not a date.* She opened her menu and ducked behind it.

Kye tugged it down with his index finger. "I recommend the fish. All fresh from the lake."

She folded her menu and laid it on the table. "Sounds great."

"So," Kye leaned forward and rested his forearm on the table, his hand close to the flickering flame.

"So," Grace leaned in and stretched out her arm but refrained from touching him. Mere millimeters separated the tips of their fingers.

"Who do you think is behind all these pranks at the camp?"

Grace slid her hands back into her lap. The pranks. They were here to discuss the pranks. It's not a date. It's a safe place to talk.

"Can I take your order?" The waiter's perfectly timed interruption gave her a minute to collect her thoughts. What Kye must think of her getting all dressed up?

Thankfully, she didn't wear the dress!

Kye ordered. "We'll both have the fish, please."

"Lovely choice." The waiter took their menus and left.

Grace focused on her lap.

"A penny for your thoughts?"

"Ah, Judy had opportunity to access your computer and hide the cinch. But I don't see her as someone who'd sink netting into the lake and potentially harm the kids." If they were here to talk business, then she'd talk business.

"I agree. Judy doesn't seem to have it in her. What about Kaleb? Or Eric? Their dad has been trying to buy the camp so he can develop it into lakefront cottages. Kaleb helped bolt together the slide that failed."

"But what would be in it for Kaleb?"

"I don't know. Maybe a cut of the profits?"

A young girl approached with a water pitcher and filled their glasses. They waited until she walked away.

"It kind of looked like him hurrying down the mountain trails after those rocks fell on me," Grace conceded.

"Yeah, but I don't know. If the saboteur unlocked the supply shed, enabling that boy to steal the canoe on the day we met, then he'd have to be willing to endanger a child.

They've both worked camps for years. I just don't see them doing that." He played with the cutlery on his napkin. "Do you think it could be a competing camp?"

"I asked Uncle Carl the same thing. He seems to think that the camps work hard to support each other, not compete."

"Shawn had access to the saddle, but could he have done the other things?"

A young man placed a bread basket on the table between them.

Kye reached across the table for her hands. "Can I ask the blessing?"

She tried to pray along in her mind, but the gentle pressure of his warm hands proved too big a distraction. As soon as he said "amen" she slipped her hands from his warm grasp and helped herself to a piece of bread. She busied herself spreading a pat of butter over it.

"Was the bear attack a fluke or another scheme to defame the camp?" she asked.

"Ron suggested someone might have lured the bear." But Kye looked unconvinced.

"Could someone do any of this?"

They sat in silence. The more they discussed it, the crazier it sounded. But they couldn't deny that too many things had gone wrong to be happenstance. Despite lacking the evidence to prove someone was scheming against the camp, they had seen the sabotage with their own eyes.

Grace's phone rang. "Hello?"

"Grace, thank goodness! Are you OK? What's going on over there?" Her mother's shrill voice carried across the table. Kye probably heard every word.

"Mom, what are you talking about? Kye and I are out for dinner."

"I'm talking about the fire trucks and flashing lights coming from the camp!"

"Fire trucks?" Grace and Kye spoke in unison.

"Yes! Camp Moshe is on fire!"

# 12

Kye thrust the car into park and spilled out the door. "Is everyone OK?" The tight huddle of Camp Moshe staff parted to let him through.

"It looks worse than it is." Bobby stepped in front of Kye and placed a hand on his chest to stop him from rushing into the building.

Everyone else shuffled back, as if uncertain how Kye would react to being stopped.

Kye looked from the hand on his chest to Bobby and back to his chest.

Bobby dropped his hand.

Kye dragged his eyes across the nightmare scene. Two firemen exited the kitchen, and several others worked together retracting hoses and cleaning up. It was far calmer than he had expected. Organized. Could the worst be over?

He focused on Bobby, now uncomfortably shifting his weight from foot to foot, still blocking his path. "No one was hurt?"

"No, sir."

"Thank you, God!" Kye's tight neck and shoulder muscles released like a ripple one tiny section at a time. He tipped his face heavenward inhaling a sweet breath of relief. This could have been bad. He rubbed the heel of one palm into his eye and swallowed hard. He had to get a grip.

He methodically met each pair of eyes watching him fight against a mental breakdown. By God's grace each person appeared unscathed.

"What happened?" Kye finally broke the quiet.

"Grease flared the minute I lit the stove so I dosed the whole thing with baking soda, but it got big fast. The smoke triggered the alarm, but I managed to put the fire out." Bobby pulled back his shoulders and puffed out his chest.

"Why was the fire department dispatched if you handled it so quickly?"

Bobby deflated. "I couldn't find the security code to halt dispatch's automatic call to them." Red crept up the sides of his face. He likely recalled that Kye gave him the code on his first day and told him to memorize it.

"Why didn't someone call me?" He raked

202

his eyes over Kate, Kaleb, Eric, and the others.

Kate turned toward the distant lake. Kaleb and Eric studied the ground like it had just sprouted magic beans. Only Bobby met his eyes.

Bobby raised his hands in front of him in mock surrender. "I tried to call you. Multiple times. You never answered."

Kye shut his eyes, reliving the earlier moment he had put his phone on silent. Never again.

"Who left the stovetop greasy?"

A droplet of sweat beaded on Bobby's forehead. Was he nervous he'd lose his job in the kitchen or was he hiding something? "I keep a clean kitchen, so I don't know. Maybe a staffer came in and made himself dinner and never cleaned up."

Bobby didn't look away and didn't blink.

Kye relented. He couldn't blame the guy for freezing up and forgetting a six-digit code. Bobby was a cook, not a first responder trained to react well under duress. He forced a smile. "Thanks for acting fast enough to prevent it from spreading."

Relief flooded Bobby's face. His entire frame relaxed.

"You don't think someone —" Grace started.

Kye silenced her with a look. He hadn't noticed Grace following him from the car, and he didn't need her spouting sabotage theories in earshot of the fire chief and in front of the camp staff. This couldn't possibly be connected to the other mishaps.

Grace's hand on his forearm pulled him back to the present scene. She slid her fingers into his and gently squeezed.

"It'll be OK," she whispered.

He wasn't sure anything would be okay ever again. Besides, she shouldn't be making impossible promises. She needed to be concerned about the camp and whoever was trying to shut it down. Until they figured out what was going on, no one was safe.

He tugged her a few steps away and dipped his head grazing her ear with his words. "Do you think this was an accident?"

Her face paled, and she visibly swallowed. Her voice lowered to match his. "It has to be. If this was on purpose, then —"

He placed his finger to her lips to hush her words. They were softer than he expected. He let his fingers linger. "Can it be another hit in a string of bad luck?"

Neither of them wanted to voice the alternative. If this was arson, their villain had considerably raised the stakes.

"What matters is that no one was hurt."

She clasped his hand and squeezed.

"But how long will we be able to say that? The campers arrive tomorrow." Assuming campers even arrived after parents got wind of this. Another round of bad press could sink their ship for sure.

The chief headed his way. Maybe now they'd get some answers. He let go of Grace's hand, and a news van rolled into the lot blocking the fire chief's path. Great.

Kye's fingers curled into his palms. Why couldn't he catch a break?

"You OK?" Grace wrapped her arms around her middle and rocked back on her heels. The breeze of the lake billowed her thin blouse as she stood beside him and studied the cameraman propping a camera on his shoulder and focusing the lens on the reporter who'd already sidelined the chief.

"I'll have to be."

They watched the interview. "So what are you going to do?"

What was he going to do? That was the million-dollar question. "I'm going to ask the chief for some advice."

"Bobby implied the stove can be repaired, and the rest of the damage is cosmetic. Maybe we won't have to go through insurance if we fix this ourselves."

The chief wrapped up with the reporter and made a beeline for Kye. The reporter caught Kye's eye and motioned she'd like to speak with him. Kye nodded and held two fingers indicating he'd need a minute.

"Malachi Campton?" The chief held out his hand for Kye to shake. "Chief Paul. Can I have a minute?"

Kye shook the chief's hand, and the staff, who had clustered off into groups of twos and threes, eagerly pressed in to listen. Bobby boldly joined Kye and Grace.

"Do you think we should cancel the first week of camp?" Bobby asked. "I mean, how are we going to get this cleaned up by tomorrow and make sure it's all safe for the kids?"

Bobby's voice carried, and the reporter looked their way again. She motioned for the cameraman to roll tape.

"Quiet down!" Kye sliced through the air with his hand. "No one is cancelling anything until after I speak with the chief."

"But —"

"But nothing," Kye interrupted.

The smile stretched across Grace's face provided the boost of confidence he needed.

Kye eyed the remaining staff and settled his gaze on Bobby. "I don't want to see any of you on the news, unless it is to say 'no

206

comment'."

"We could always add firefighting to the extreme camp experience." Bobby laughed at his own joke while the others groaned. He gave Kaleb a good-natured punch to the arm.

The chief frowned.

Was Bobby being funny, or was that glint in his eye a challenge?

"Let's get to work cleaning up." Bobby slapped his hands together and rallied the troops before Kye could decide.

A tight smile stretched Kye's features. For now, he had no choice but to trust the men and women he'd hired to do their jobs. But from here on out, he was watching all of them. Closely.

The staff disbanded, providing Kye and the chief a private minute.

"There are some things here that don't add up."

Kye's pulse spiked. "Like what?"

"All fires need three things: oxygen, a fuel source, and heat. In arson cases, one of those items has been tampered with."

"This was arson?" Kye looked around. Every TV show he had ever seen that involved an arsonist said the villain watched his fires. Was he here now? Watching?

"I suspect the fuel load was increased —"

Kye snapped his attention back to Paul. "Can you please explain in layman terms?"

"Someone introduced flammable material or an accelerant."

"Are you sure?"

"I can't say for certain. I wasn't able to collect sufficient evidence, but my gut tells me something is going on here." The chief's words carried a sharp edge. His tone implied this had been no ordinary fire. A lack of evidence didn't prove innocence. Paul trusted his gut enough to warn Kye.

The word *accelerant* looped in his mind. Grace and Bobby organized the clean-up a few feet away, assigning various responsibilities. What did he know about his staff? He recalled their applications. Nothing looked suspicious, but when he'd been hiring he hadn't been trying to smoke out a rat.

Paul followed his gaze. "That your staff over there?"

"Yes. And we have campers arriving to-morrow. What do you recommend?"

"Sleeping with one eye open."

Grace looked at each eager face glowing in the flickering campfire flames. The campers had arrived without a hitch, got themselves settled into their assigned cabins, and had just finished cooking s'mores over the fire pit. Kye said he fielded surprisingly few calls from concerned parents following the news report of the fire. It had been officially listed as accidental, and the reporter even praised Bobby for his quick thinking in smothering it with baking soda.

Grace stood in a horizontal line of staff members, waiting for her turn to explain the water electives and what participants could expect from her this week. Right now, Eric and Kaleb tag-teamed telling rock-climbing stories.

"One time Kaleb was rappelling down a mountain and he reached a cliff —"

"Aw, don't tell that one," Kaleb cut in. "It's too embarrassing."

"Tell us! Tell us!" the kids chanted.

"Kaleb reached a cliff edge and lowered himself into a seated position." Eric shot his brother a grin, and Kaleb dropped his head in mock shame. "He didn't see the cactus under him."

The kids howled.

"It was the kind with many small thorns," Kaleb solemnly added.

"My dad and I had to pick the thorns from his bottom with tweezers," Eric finished.

When the kids calmed down, Eric assured

them there were no cacti in Northern Ontario.

The rapt expressions on the kid's faces made Grace's stomach roll. The climbing program would be full.

Kye stood off to the side, observing. He folded his arms across his chest and scanned the kids looking a bit like a proud parent. And he should be proud. It had been a hard run getting here, but now that the camp season had officially begun, maybe whoever had been trying to shut the place down would admit defeat and cease?

A girl could hope.

When Kye scanned the staff, his eyes noticeably darkened. Like he didn't know who he could trust.

Why the wariness? This moment should feel pretty victorious. Less than twenty-four hours ago the place was crawling with firemen and now it was crawling with happy kids about to embark on some crazy adventures.

She pushed that aside.

What was Kye's problem?

He caught her eye and his expression softened.

She winked.

His gaze lingered on her a moment too long, and a few *oohs* rumbled through the pre-teens nearest to her.

A blush heated her cheeks. So much for rapt attention on Eric and Kaleb.

Two snickering boys poked at each other and whispered while casting conniving glances around. She frowned. Having been a camper herself, she recognized the mischievous spark in their eyes.

"Thank you, Eric and Kaleb." Kye led the campers in applause. "Now, Kate will explain the hands-on, not-your-normal-camp-craft experience, awaiting those majoring in crafts."

Kye directed everyone's attention to Kate who moved front and center and held up a piece of driftwood intricately engraved. "Those of you who choose the wood-burning elective will scavenge for driftwood . . ."

Grace slipped out of line and circled behind the gathering to tap Kye on the shoulder.

"Yes?"

"See those two boys there?" She nodded at the brown-headed, gangly pre-teens perched on a log by the fire a few feet away from the rest of their cabin crew. Their heads bent close together, drawing some sort of map or scheme into the dirt with a stick.

He followed her head nod. "I see them."

"Watch out for them. I have a feeling they have a few camp tricks up their sleeves."

He smirked. "Relax. They're kids. It'll be fine."

"Famous last words," she chuckled. "Don't say I didn't warn you."

Kye studied her.

"What?" Did she have graham cracker crumbs in her teeth?

"I like hearing you laugh. With everything that's happened, I haven't heard it much."

She tucked a loose strand of hair around her ear. "Now camp's started, I feel like I can finally breathe."

He quizzically raised his brows.

"Running my program is one of several steps I need to complete to qualify for a government grant. If I win the grant, I can expand and train more instructors than just Debbie."

"That would be wonderful." A genuine smile spread across his face forcing his dimples to pucker into his cheeks.

"If things go according to plan, I could have my program in schools as early as the New Year."

"That's really important to you, isn't it?"

Her eyes filled but she blinked back the tears. "I need to properly honor the memory of my dad and sister. Maybe then I'll find the peace I need to move on."

"I'll be praying you do." Kye gave her hand a brief squeeze before stepping forward and introducing Grace.

She slipped back into line just as Kye announced her title as the Director of Water Activities. Grace succinctly summarized the offered lifeguarding certification program, Water Survival for Non-Swimmers, boat licensing, water skiing, and other typical water-based activities.

Kye led the group in appreciative applause.

The shorter boy Grace had warned Kye about snorted and elbowed his buddy.

Grace stepped back into line. These boys were going to make the first week of camp quite the adventure. She was sure of it.

The next morning the sun rose early. Grace stood half asleep in the breakfast line wishing she had gotten herself a coffee first. At least she didn't have a crew of kids to contend with. As a director, she enjoyed a cabin to herself. Her night had to have been far more restful than the cabin leaders'.

Eric slid into line behind her.

"Good morning."

"What's so good about it?" He snagged a plate and shuffled down the buffet.

"What, you're not fond of pancakes?"

"No, I like pancakes fine. I'm just not fond of short-sheeted beds and put-the-sleeping-cabin-leader's-hand-in-a-bucket-of-warm-water-to-make-him-pee-in-his-sleeping-bag trick."

Grace gasped. Then she laughed so hard kids turned in their chairs to discover the source of the noise.

"You think that's funny?" Kate piped up from behind. Dark smudges shadowed her eyes. "There was a snake in our cabin. By the time we got it out of there, none of the girls would sleep." She shuddered.

Grace tried to suppress her giggling, but these two had no idea what kind of summer was in store for them. One of the job requirements should have been previous camping experience. "Sorry to break it to you, but the fun has only just begun."

Grace scooped up a stack of pancakes, called a thanks to Bobby in the kitchen, and headed toward Kye's table. She sat down across from him. Hopefully his night went better.

"How did you sleep?"

He smiled. "Good, considering how many kids are here."

"No homesick kiddos making late night calls to mom and dad? No bears slinking around cabins?"

"None yet." He stabbed a slice of bacon. "And I doubt we'll ever have to worry about bears. If the noise doesn't scare them off, the smell certainly will."

"Ah, the aroma of youthful boys in the summer. You never quite get used to it."

"Youth that need a lesson in hygiene." Kye wrinkled his nose.

A chuckle bubbled out of her. "Once they get into the lake, it'll dissipate." Grace was familiar with all the sounds and smells of boyhood, thanks to Jeremy.

She repeated the tales she had heard from Eric and Kate, pleased to see some of yesterday's tension had lifted from his eyes.

"I'll take cabin pranks over sabotage any day." He leaned back in his chair sipping his coffee. "Hey, aren't those the boys you warned me about?"

Grace caught the tail end of the duo sneaking past the window. They must have come from the trail that led from the boat shed. She pushed back her chair. "I'm gonna see what they're up to."

"Wait for me." Kye deposited their trays in the proper place and followed her outside. They parted ways where the path forked.

"Call me if anything is missing or rigged

to explode." His lips turned up at the corners.

"You can count on it."

Acting on the assumption that the boys were up to no good, she took a methodical inventory of the boat shed. Sure enough, her CPR dolls were missing. A quick search uncovered them on display in the park perched on the see-saw as if they were enjoying the ride. She snapped a few pictures and texted them to Kye.

*See what they did?*

*That doesn't look rigged to explode,* he texted back.

*Lol, at least it was nothing serious.*

Or so she thought.

She stepped through the trees and saw the pier jutting out into the deep water. It held a mini platform with an extended diving board. They had cling-wrapped a kayak to the board. Not cool.

A few pictures and forty-five minutes later, Grace had the boys in Kye's office standing before him.

"We didn't hurt anyone. What's the big deal?" The larger boy, Deacon, defiantly stood his ground. Will, the younger of the two, and likely the more easily influenced, looked scared. He probably thought they'd call his mother.

"The big deal is that you could have fallen into the lake and hurt yourself. That kayak is expensive and the water is off-limits without supervision." Kye shot them such a severe look that Grace's knees knocked. She'd have to remember to compliment him on his enforcer glare.

Kye stared them down. The boys shifted their body weight from side to side. "We're sorry. We won't do it again."

"Were you behind last night as well?" Grace cut in, not ready to let them completely off the hook.

Their eyebrows hit the roof.

"We know about the trick on Eric, and the snake in the girls' cabin."

"We wanted to see if we could get someone to go home on the first night." The whine in Deacon's voice set her teeth on edge. Talk about a boy only a mother could love.

Kye's cell vibrated on the desktop and shattered the confession. "Kye here."

Grace stared at the boys. Clearly her enforcer glare wasn't as scary. Deacon stared right back.

"What? Stay right there. I'm on my way." Kye pushed back his office chair and stood.

"What's going on?"

"There's some trouble on the bike trail."

He shot the boys a look.

Deacon backed up a step. "Hey, don't look at us. We're here with you!"

"This isn't over," Kye promised. "For now, go find your cabin mates and join the activities."

The boys left. They weren't ten steps away before their heads bent together with furious whispers bouncing between them.

Kye held the door for Grace. "Are you coming with me?"

"You bet. Jeremy is in that group." She paused in the doorway. "Just curious, do you still prefer cabin pranks?"

# 13

Kye slapped away branches as he led the way down a mountain trail so narrow they had to walk single file. "The bikers are just up here."

"It's a bit further out than I thought." Grace kept pace like a trooper. Was she tired, or put out over the time it was taking to reach the kids? He slapped his forehead. Her electives. Why hadn't he considered that she had her own electives to run?

He turned around and she bumped into him. He briefly caught her forearms and steadied her. "Are you OK for time? When do you need to be in the water?"

"I've got a few hours." She swatted a low-slung branch. "I might like a cold morning swim, but most others don't. I scheduled my classes for afternoon and evenings when the campers would most enjoy the lake."

"Good. The path widens soon." Kye continued to hike, thankful Grace was behind him and unable to read his expressions. She had become so easy to be with he sometimes forgot she wasn't here to help him. They weren't partners, or even a couple. She had her own agenda — getting her program off the ground to honor her family. She'd been very clear that until she succeeded, she had no interest in anything else. Sure, they'd become friends, but ultimately, he was a means to an end.

He'd remind himself of that more often.

After five more minutes, an inconspicuous storage shed built into the edge of the woods came into view. It was well camouflaged. Most people would hike right by it never knowing that within a stone's throw were hidden trail bikes, repair kits, first aid supplies, and an emergency two-way radio connected to Judy at the front office desk.

Kye had the shed built when he added mountain biking to the camp electives. He purposefully chose to roof and side it in natural material found in the woods to keep it as unobtrusive as possible.

"What's going on?" Kye and Grace entered the clearing just past the shed that marked the beginning of the trail where ten kids crowded around Jon, one of the trail leaders, and his assistant leader, Nick.

Jon stooped over a bike, fiddling with the

mechanics. A dozen more bikes littered the ground in various stages of repair.

"An impromptu lesson in bike repair and safety checks." Jon stood and wiped his greasy hands on his denim shorts.

"Impromptu?" Grace repeated.

"While doing our pre-ride screening I noticed many of the bolts had been loosened. I didn't want to take any chances, so we're carefully going over each bike."

"This happened to me once." Jeremy paused from tightening a nut near the back wheel and looked up. "My dad bought a preassembled bike but the clerk never tightened the nuts. The wheel fell off as dad took it out of the trunk."

Kye squatted to study one bicycle while Grace went to Jeremy to look over the bike he planned to ride. "Is that what happened here?"

Jon lowered his voice. "No. I assembled all these myself and they were secure."

The saboteur was back.

Kye returned to the shed and examined the door and the lock. "Did this look tampered with?" It wasn't impossible for someone to find the shed. The trails were open to everyone. But considering it was a new build made it very unlikely.

Grace and Jon joined him, putting a bit of

distance between them and the kids. Nick kept the kids occupied by giving step-by-step repair instructions.

"No, everything seemed normal," Jon said. "Thankfully it's nothing serious, but it could have been."

"If one of these kids had been going downhill —"

"I know, Grace. I don't need that now."

A wounded look flashed through her eyes. She subtly shifted her body away from him.

"Grace," he tugged on her elbow. He didn't intend to be harsh, but the last thing he needed was false hysteria building on 'what if' scenarios. They had enough trouble without borrowing more.

She shook her head. "No, you're right. We need to focus."

He appreciated her change of heart, but something in her tone sent ripples of wariness through him. She avoided eye contact.

Why was this hitting her so hard? Because Jeremy was here?

He faced Jon. This job definitely didn't turn out to be the cushy summer breeze he'd hoped for. "Do you feel like you have it under control?"

"Yeah, we got it all fixed. Checking the bikes is part of our normal routine."

Maybe whoever did this knew that and

didn't intend to hurt anyone. Maybe they just wanted to subtly remind him the threat remained. The fire chief's warning replayed in his brain and a sick sensation rolled through his gut. He had a horrible feeling that whatever this was, it was nowhere close to being over.

He let out a controlled breath. "OK, continue on as planned, but be extra cautious until we figure out what is happening."

Jon nodded. "No worries. I rode the trail first thing this morning to ensure there were no new trees down or anything, and it was fine. When we ride, I'm in the front and Nick follows behind to make sure we don't lose anyone. We'll be fine."

"Thanks for calling me." Kye turned to Grace. "Ready?"

She nodded stiffly. "You're the boss." She scooted to Jeremy, whispered a few words into his ears, and then headed back down the trail ahead of Kye.

Jon smirked at her retreating back. "Have a nice walk back."

Kye rushed to catch up with her. Her stiff posture briefly reminded him of his mother when she didn't get her way. It soured his stomach. Whether Grace liked it or not, he was the boss.

"Grace!"

She turned, cheeks damp and eyes bright. Fear etched on her face.

"Grace," he softened. "Jeremy will be fine. You have to trust that I know what I'm doing."

"What if this is the same creep who loosened my cinch? What if it's not fine?"

"What do you suggest? We give up and close shop?"

"I can't, Kye. Next year I won't qualify for the grant."

Of course. It was all about her program. Kye's phone dinged. "Just a minute."

Grace wrapped her arms around her middle and rubbed her hands up and down her arms for warmth.

Kye tapped his messages and opened an email attachment. Tony sent the new numbers. His stomach hit the dirt. "No," he choked out.

Grace's eyes widened.

His thumbs frantically worked his phone, opening each attachment. He added the numbers in his head and fought against bile rising in his throat. He slapped his palm against the tree, turned his back against it, and slid to the ground clutching his head. "This can't be happening."

"What's wrong?" Grace followed him, her

words laced with alarm.

His stomach churned. How could he tell her? She'd been counting on him. Everyone had been counting on him.

"Kye, you're scaring me."

This was his fault. Guilt gut-stabbed him. He'd let his friendship with Grace cloud his focus and he had no one to blame but himself. If he'd been on his A-game, he would have seen this coming and prepared for it.

"We can't afford the new insurance premiums."

"What?" she moved closer. "What does that mean?"

"The first payment cleared, but the increase is so big that even with a full enrollment, we'll end the season in the red."

"And that means . . ." her voice trailed off. He'd never told her that if the numbers projected a certain deficit the board would have to sell. They had already run in the red for two years, and when they updated the cabins and kitchen to meet new health and safety regulations, it drained their savings. They planned to close the doors rather than see another year accumulate more debt.

"It means that the camp will never be viable without a serious rate hike."

"So hike the rates for the rest of the summer." She shrugged as if it were that simple.

"But the majority of our kids come from low-income families. We can apply to foundations for grants to fund future years, but that won't help this one."

"So what does that mean for us right now?"

"It means if we don't clear this year in the black, there may not *be* any future years. If we can't prove to the board that we can carry these insurance increases until funding kicks in, this may be our one and only week of camp."

Disbelief contorted her face. She pulled back from him, shaking her head. "How much more can it be? Didn't you expect an increase?"

"Yes, I did. But I didn't expect Tony to overhear you and me talking about the rock climbing mishap and debating the safety merits of the camp elective. Added to the damage left by the bear and him witnessing your fall off the horse, well, he ranked us as very high-risk."

As though a dam had burst, her words surged. "I knew it was a bad idea. I knew it. How could you do this, Kye? I thought you were Mr. Fix-it and proud of it?"

Every word pounded another nail of guilt into him. "I didn't rig your cinch. I didn't lure the bear and I didn't insist on talking about rock climbing while Tony was here."

"You're blaming me?" He wouldn't have thought her tanned complexion could have paled further, but it did. Two flaming circles of righteous indignation flooded her cheeks and popped in stark contrast to her white flesh.

"No, I'm not blaming you." Because it was his fault. He let Grace get close. He let her have a stronger voice than she should have, and that influenced his decisions. If he'd kept his distance, he would have seen the camp's forecast and pulled out before the board invested more cash. But the thought of letting her down when she needed this so much had muddied the waters. He forgot what he was here to do: protect the interests of the investors, not play hero to Grace. Now everyone would have to pay.

A small part of him had hoped she was different from Annette, even different than his mother. But her reaction proved she was just like every girl he'd ever known. She played nice while things went her way, but her attitude changed with the current.

"Uh, guys? I don't mean to interrupt, but Judy told me I could find you out here." Bobby uncomfortably inched around the corner of the trail. Clearly, he'd heard every word they said.

"Yes?" Kye stifled a sigh.

"I'm guessing this isn't the best time to tell you, but someone added Ex-Lax to the brownie batter."

Kye's strength drained. "Do I need to come?"

"No, but I thought you'd want to know considering, you know . . ." His voice trailed off. When neither Kye nor Grace responded, he turned to head back to camp.

"Hey, wait up. We're going back too." Kye jogged to catch up and motioned for Grace to follow. Maybe having a witness would help him and Grace weigh their words.

"You know, I couldn't help but overhear you say the camp might close?" Bobby snuck a sheepish look at Kye. "I didn't mean to listen in or anything, but you guys were pretty loud."

"I might as well tell you. I'll be announcing it later anyway. We're short the funds needed to pay the insurance. Once I tell the board we'll likely end the season in debt, they'll vote on a standing offer to purchase the camp."

"There's a standing offer to purchase?"

"Yeah. Kaleb and Eric's dad wants to build some new lakefront cottages."

"You know," Bobby said, "a lot of staff are

counting on these jobs for school and stuff. Maybe we could all buy a few shares? I'd gladly forfeit a paycheck if it secured the rest for the summer. I bet the others would too. Would that give you enough to see the summer out?"

Kye considered the idea. "It's worth considering."

"Have you forgotten what Uncle Carl said?" Grace cut in. "When they discussed selling shares before, they rejected the idea."

"But that was when one person wanted to buy a majority. If these shares are small enough, then the board members would still maintain control." It was a solid idea worth presenting.

"There has to be a better way to save the camp," Grace insisted.

Was she worried about the camp? Or just her program?

Kye was no longer sure.

"So here's the deal. The camp needs a large sum of money to pay for the unexpected insurance increases this year. If we cannot raise these funds, the board will vote to decide if they should close Camp Moshe as early as the end of the week." Grace couldn't help but notice how Kye's eyes skipped her as he briefly paused on each staff member.

If anybody on staff arrived sleepy from the early morning hour, sleep dissipated the minute his words passed his lips. Disbelief rolled through the crowd like a tidal wave. Murmurs of college costs and unfairness crested the conversations reminding Grace she wasn't the only one Kye had let down.

If he'd spent more time crunching numbers like he was supposed to, maybe he would've caught this in time.

But was that fair? A tiny nugget of guilt ate her insides. She'd been the distraction. Memories of her flouncing into his office in that self-made anti-bear getup, accepting lunch invitations from his mother, swimming together, and that tender moment at the top of Mount Yahweh-Yireh flooded her mind. She pushed them down. It wasn't about fair. Nothing in her life had been fair. Especially getting this close to her dream of funding Water Survival for Non-Swimmers and losing it.

"Can we do something to raise the cash?" Eric asked.

Kye rubbed the back of his neck. "Bobby had an idea about staff buying shares, but we'd have to convince the board there were enough of you willing to participate to raise enough money, but the more I think about it, the less I like the idea. We don't want to overreact and lose permanent shares trying to fix a temporary problem."

"Maybe we can have a community BBQ or start a crowdfunding webpage," suggested Grace.

"I've managed crowdfunding pages before," said Kate.

"There are a lot of people who believe in this camp." Grace stepped into the center of the meeting. "I know if we worked together, we'd be able to save this place."

"I'm not sure we could pull that off in time." Bobby shook his head. "I don't know about the rest of you, but if I'm out of a job next week, I need to know now — not after a failed funding page or a community potluck. I stand by my share idea."

Bobby didn't have the same connection to this place as Grace, the same history. She stiffened her frame. "I believe in this place and I won't go down without a fight." The others might all be able to walk away unscathed, losing nothing more than a summer job, but she'd have lost her last chance to qualify for the grant.

"Sounds like an uphill battle, but to each his own." Bobby shrugged and blended back in with the other staff.

"Would any of you have a problem if I tried anyway?" It wouldn't be the first time she had to swim upstream alone. She scanned the crowd, skipping Kye like he had skipped her. She didn't want to read any negativity in his eyes.

"No? That settles it. Kate, will you set up that funding page?"

Kate nodded.

"Great, I'll get the word out about the BBQ. We can have it in two days, on Friday night. I'll ask for pledges from the families who have had life-changing encounters with God here at Camp Moshe."

The group disbanded.

She felt the weight of Kye's stare. After his speech, he had pulled back to the edges and simply watched his staff process the announcement. Should she go to him? Try to smooth over their rough edges? Before she could decide, Bobby approached him gesturing passionately.

"Are you going to the board to present the share idea or are you going to wait and see how Grace's scheme plays out?"

"I'll include all the suggestions in my presentation on Friday."

"Your opinion really matters, right?"

"I give a recommendation, but ultimately, it is up to them."

"So what will you recommend?"

He rubbed his neck. "It's not what you

want to hear, but I'm leaning toward advising against the share idea. In the long run, we have a higher risk of losing control. All we need is a temporary solution until we can increase prices or get more funding."

Grace's conscience pinched. Kye's business decisions seemed so logical and well-reasoned compared to her emotional response.

Kye lightly punched Bobby's arm. "Don't look so bummed. It was a good idea, just not the best one for this camp."

Bobby's smile was forced. "What time do you meet?"

"We meet right before my flight to Phoenix."

"Phoenix? You're leaving? Now?"

"My company insisted I check the next job, especially since it looks like this one could end ahead of schedule." He raked his fingers through his hair like he always did when he was troubled.

A sympathetic pang hit her heart, but she hardened herself. He had choices, but he was putting his career before Camp Moshe.

"Don't they need you here to — I don't know — wrap things up?"

She stiffened. Did Kye know she could hear them?

Kye looked away and for a nanosecond

their gazes collided, then he shifted his attention back to Bobby but couldn't hide the emotional hitch in his voice.

"My trip is a fact-finding trip. And they threatened to drop me if I didn't go. Besides, if the board decides to sell the camp, there'll be nothing for me here."

Would he stay if she gave him a reason?

Bobby's phone vibrated. "Yeah?" He motioned good-bye and turned to leave. His faint voice carried over as he stomped away. "You promised. I need it by tomorrow. You don't understand —"

Kye's lingering gaze churned her stomach. What did he expect from her? For her to accept failure? To abandon her goals and her dreams just because he said it was over?

Whatever had sparked between them had died. It was bound to anyway. It's not like she could follow him around from place to place as he played hero conquering the business world. She wanted, needed to establish her program and put down roots.

It just wasn't meant to be.

She subtly turned her back to him. He had another job all lined up and nothing but a single black mark on his resume. She lost everything. Well, she wasn't giving up that easily. There were enough people who believed in this camp. If they worked together, they could save it. She was sure of it.

She trudged to the water's edge and stripped off her outer layer. Her regular morning swim would help clear her thoughts. And at least in the water, no one would be able to see her tears.

She waded out, feeling small in the vast expanse. Every stroke away from shore tied a weight to her feet and threatened to tug her under. She hadn't felt this alone since her dad and sister died. So small that God couldn't find her. So lost from Him. She swiped at her tears and turned around to head back to shore. For the first time, a swim didn't help.

Kye waited on the beach. The crowd had thinned until only he remained in the early morning sunshine. Something changed between them when he admitted his failure. Like beach sand through her fingers, their friendship slipped away with their lost common goal. She didn't know whether to feel relieved or sad.

But no matter what, she couldn't avoid him forever. Especially since he waited by her discarded clothing.

She staggered to the beach.

"We need to talk." The thin line of his lips implied this might be unpleasant.

"Yeah, I guess we do." Especially since he planned to jump ship later this week and start a cushy job in Phoenix. He didn't believe she could save the camp. He was giving up without even trying.

"I'm not convinced a BBQ is enough to save the camp. I'd hate to see you get your hopes up for them to only be dashed."

"Didn't you tell me to get on board or get out?"

That took him aback.

"You know, back in the beginning, when I questioned your methods?"

"I just don't want to see you get hurt." He stretched out a hand to touch her arm, but she stepped out of reach.

"I'm going to save this place. You need to decide if you're going to help, or just follow corporate orders."

"What?"

"It's simple, Kye. Get on board, or get out."

She turned on her heel and stomped away. Kye wasn't the only person who could fix things around here.

# 14

Grace flipped over the paper on her clipboard and held it down with her hand. The wind caught the free corner and flapped it back and forth. She crossed off another item on her to-do list. Everything had come together for the BBQ. All they needed now was for the weather to cooperate.

She shaded her eyes and studied the clouds. Tendrils of hair worked loose and tickled her cheeks. It could go either way. *Please God. Hold back the rain.*

"Well that was the last of the campers." Kate approached, wiping her hands together as if dusting them off.

"Everyone has gone home?"

"All picked up, happily reunited with their parents after an exciting week at camp." She paused as if weighing her next words. She forged ahead in one breath. "Kye wanted to know if you needed anything for tonight?"

If she needed anything? Just for him to

believe in this place. To believe in her.

"Grace?" Kate's warm hand on her arm tugged her back into the present moment.

"No. Tell him I've got everything I need."

Kate's disapproval was clear, but Grace didn't owe her an explanation. She and Kye were never an official item. Grace cleared her throat. "So how's that crowdfunding page coming along?"

Kate brightened. "Great. But we only have about a third of the money we need. Many of the families you were in touch with funded the Camp Moshe page. Hopefully, we'll get more tonight."

Grace forced a smile. They'd have to get more money tonight if they were going to save the camp. She'd never admit it, but it was starting to look like Kye was right. A BBQ was never going to be enough to save Camp Moshe.

Bobby waved Kate over from the picnic table where he was setting up. "Looks like Bobby could use some help," Grace said.

Kate headed over and Grace put on a brave face as she smiled and waved at Bobby. She couldn't let the staff down. They were depending on their summer jobs.

"Grace! Grace!"

Grace turned, and Jeremy nearly knocked her over. She grabbed his arm to steady them both. "Are you OK?"

"I'm fine," he huffed. "You'll never guess what I found."

He held out a shiny gold nugget and puffed out his chest. "I found gold on the trails! This'll fix everything! We'll be rich!"

Jeremy's squeal caught Bobby and Kate's attention; concern darkened Bobby's eyes.

She waved at him and mouthed the words, *it's OK*. It was sweet the way he cared about Jeremy's feelings.

Grace slipped her arm around her brother's shoulder and tugged him aside, not wanting to embarrass the boy. "Are you sure it's not pyrite?" She hated to burst his youthful enthusiasm, but she'd been fooled by fool's gold more than once as a kid in these very woods.

"What's that?"

"It's called fool's gold. It's fake. See here," she pointed to the edges. "Fool's gold has sharp edges and it separates into layers. It's very angular. Real gold has rounder edges and it shines in any light, not just when the sun catches it right."

Jeremy studied the nugget, tilting it in the sunlight that managed to peek through the gathering clouds.

A pang hit her chest as she remembered her dad teaching her sister and her about fool's gold the last summer they had together at this camp. She wasn't much younger than Jeremy was now.

Jeremy huffed and reddened.

"It's nothing to be embarrassed about. Looks enough like the real deal to even fool some adults."

"Easy for you to say. You're not the one jumping and hollering about a dumb rock."

"Hey, Uncle Carl has told me about lots of adults fooled by pyrite. It's not just kids. Besides," she turned Jeremy around. "There is no one here but you, me, and Kate. And Kate isn't paying us any attention. And even if she did, you've known her for years. She's like another sister." Thankfully, Bobby had left the area.

"Yeah, I guess."

"Well I think it's a pretty cool find." A low rumble rolled through the sky, and the wind snapped at the tent tops lining the beach. At least they had tents for anyone committed enough to Camp Moshe to venture out on a gloomy day. "Maybe you should head back. Mom'll be worried if it starts to storm and you're outside."

"Aw, it'll pass. This always happens around the lake."

"I hope you're right."

Her phone rang, and the caller I.D. identified Bobby. "Hey, weren't you just here?" she laughed.

"Yeah, I was coming to talk with you, but didn't want to interrupt you and your brother. Looked kind of intense. I think I figured out who's behind everything that has been happening to us. Meet me at the blue entrance on Klymer Trail and I'll explain when you get here."

"Really?" Her heart jumped. This was huge. She hadn't been able to shake the feeling their saboteur wasn't finished and the possibility of him targeting the BBQ remained a real threat. She looked at her watch. "I don't know. The BBQ is starting soon —"

"Trust me; you'll want to see this before the BBQ and before the camp board meets. It changes things."

Her mind spun. Changed what? The camp or her fundraising plans? "OK. Have you called Kye? He'll want to know." Maybe if Kye went, she wouldn't have to.

"Yeah, he's on his way. But trust me; you're going to want to see this for yourself."

"Be there in ten." She slipped her phone back into her pocket. "Sorry Jer, but I gotta go."

"OK." He flipped the gold nugget over

and studied the backside before squinting up at her. "Are you sure, Grace?"

She ruffled his hair. "I'm sure. Sorry about the disappointment."

"Oh well. It's still cool." He stuffed it into his pocket.

"I gotta meet Bobby, but I'll be back in time for the BBQ."

In ten minutes she waited at the fork on the blue trail entrance trying to slow her racing mind. What could Bobby have found on the trails that revealed the culprit? Footsteps rustled on the path. Finally!

Kye strode around a bush, hands stuffed into his pockets, head dipped against the wind that was gaining strength.

Her heart skipped a betraying beat.

Kye nodded her way, and as the physical distance between them closed, the emotional distance stretched. He'd made his choice when he stopped believing in Camp Moshe, and it pierced her heart.

"Bobby isn't here yet," she blurted.

"I see that." The corners of his mouth tipped. "Did he tell you what he found?"

"No, just that it's huge."

They stood together, but not together. She didn't think they'd be together-together ever again. Uncomfortable minutes piled up. Grace looked at her watch and studied the bits of the darkening sky through the trees while Kye played with his phone. *Where was Bobby?*

Finally, the sound of someone jogging up the path broke the awkward silence.

"Bobby! What happened to your face?" Bobby's left eye had swollen into a slit and his ripped shirt exposed reddened skin that would likely turn a nice shade of purple by morning.

"I, uh, ran into some trouble," Bobby huffed.

"Was it him? Did our guy jump you on the trail?" Kye looked down the path after Bobby. "Did he get away? Is he still following you?"

"Did you see him? Who is it?" Grace instinctively moved closer to Kye, who rested a protective hand on the small of her back, a feathering touch that jolted her like lightning throughout the sky.

"I never saw the guy. I don't know if it's our creep or not, but if he knows I'm on to him, then we'd better hurry before he destroys the evidence."

"What if he's gone ahead? Are we safe?" Grace's eyes darted from the path to the woods to the caves ahead on the trail. If someone wanted to harm them, there were plenty of places to hide.

Kye curled his hand around her waist and gave a reassuring squeeze. "I won't let anything happen to you."

How could he still say that? He'd already inflicted the deepest wound himself by not believing in her or fighting harder for Camp Moshe.

Bobby brushed past them both and headed down the blue trail. "It's this way."

They scrambled to catch up.

Bobby appeared to favor his right leg. She reached out to him, gently brushing his shoulder with her fingertips.

He jerked around, hands fisted.

Kye thrust between them. "What's your problem?"

Bobby dropped his hands to his side. "Sorry. I'm just a bit edgy."

She exchanged a look with Kye, who shrugged. She'd probably be edgy too if someone had jumped her on the path.

"You never said anything about a hike," Grace grumbled as the incline gently increased toward a crest and then declined.

"Do you want to find the guy or not?"

Bobby's irritated tone chastised Grace. After all, he had taken a beating from the villain. The least she could do was go see the evidence.

"I have a meeting and a flight to catch. I

don't have time for this." Kye fiddled with his phone.

Of course Kye didn't have time for this. His brain had already shifted to his job in Phoenix. That only confirmed the need to continue with Bobby. If Kye wasn't committed enough to solve their mystery, she'd do it herself.

"Great, I just lost reception." Kye stuffed it into his pocket.

"You won't get any reception out this far." Bobby didn't look back.

"What's the ETA on wherever you're taking us?"

Bobby stopped and whirled around, wincing at the pain the motion caused. Anger shot out from his one good eye. "I could have left you guys to your plans and let this dude win, but I didn't. The least you could do is give me fifteen more minutes."

He was right. "I'm sorry, Bobby. We'll stop complaining." She pointed a look at Kye.

They slowly descended the mountainous terrain in silence. Bobby finally stopped them at a point where the trail hiked up a steep incline. "See here." He pointed out the blue paint marking the trees and rocks upward. "If we kept following the marked trails, we'd miss it. I only found it because I wandered off to explore down there." He indicated down through the thicker branches where all the trees looked the same. He stepped off the path.

Kye hesitated and blocked Grace from following. "If the trail isn't marked, how do you know where to go?"

Grace fought against a smirk. "Is Mr. Fix-it afraid of catching a little poison ivy?"

"No," his sharp retort bit her conscience.

"Sorry," she muttered. "That was uncalled for."

"Why can't you just tell us what you found? I'd hate to see us get lost, especially when you have a pile of guests arriving, and I have a meeting and flight to catch."

Of course that was the reason. He had a flight to catch and a new job to explore.

"It's fine," Bobby assured them. "I was just here. See how I whacked aside the bushes."

"Weren't you just at the BBQ site setting tables?" Grace frowned.

"I meant before that."

As Bobby led them further off the marked path, the intensity of the hike increased. They fell in single file — Bobby leading, Grace in the middle, Kye in the rear.

After another five minutes, she longed for her hiking boots back in her cabin but was too proud to admit her feet ached. She slowed.

"Are you OK?"

The question came from behind and brushed against her ears.

"I'm fine." She hurried to catch up to Bobby and stomped down in soft mud. Her foot slipped.

Kye shot out his arm and caught her. Their eyes met, and this time they held.

"Thank you."

Something powerful zipped between them, something that she had been trying to deny these last two days while she stewed in anger. She couldn't look away.

Kye broke the moment. "How much further?" he called ahead. He dropped her arm and she instantly missed how safe she felt with him touching her.

"Not far."

The temperature dipped at least ten degrees as they continued their descent into the heart of the rock. The damp walls emitted a chill hard to shake. Bobby finally stopped at the edge of a cliff that hovered over further depths more difficult to descend. "It's down there painted on the rock wall."

"Painted on the wall?" Kye echoed.

"It's graffiti. Like a tag."

They caught up and peered over the precipice. "How did you get down there?" she asked.

He shrugged. "I was hiking. That's not important. What matters is that our answer to everything is at the bottom of this rock."

Grace tiptoed closer to the edge.

"Be careful, Grace," Kye warned. He then turned to Bobby. "Why didn't you just take a picture of it with your cell phone and save us this long hike?" He didn't sound as if he was buying Bobby's story. "Why did you really bring us here?"

The severe drop to the bottom sent Grace's heart pounding. She backed up a step. A faint drizzle of rain made the edge slippery. "How do we get down there?"

"Carefully." Bobby started picking his way around the edge of the slippery cliff where the decline was the gentlest, but still bordered an extreme drop. He couldn't possibly expect them to —

"Something doesn't feel right about this," Kye whispered into her ear.

"If he's going down it can't be a trap, can it? Is that what you're thinking? Do you think Bobby . . . ?"

"I don't know," Kye interrupted. "We don't need to risk injury getting down there."

"But look at him." Bobby slowly moved down the dangerous edge. "I mean it's not like he beat himself up. And why would the bad guy jump a partner? It makes no sense."

"Maybe we should call the police to investigate." Kye's suggestion made sense, except Grace didn't want to wait for the police if this information was going to affect the board meeting or the outcome of the BBQ like Bobby had earlier implied.

"There isn't time," she insisted. She moved toward Bobby and ignored her heart thundering through her body as she recalled her mishap the last time she climbed these rocks. "I'm going down. We need pictures."

"Let Bobby get the pictures and bring them back."

She hesitated a half beat. Saving Camp Moshe was more important than her silly fears. If Kye didn't have a plane to catch, he'd be all over this.

She brushed past Bobby with false bravado. Less than two steps away the ground gave way and loose rocks and dirt pulled her over the edge.

"Ahh!"

Bobby clamped down on her forearm as she slid over the brink. Her body weight yanked him to the ground and he cried out on impact. His upper half hung over the cliff as he held her full weight.

She scrambled for a footing but the slippery mud and damp walls provided nothing of substance. She dangled, fully dependent, looking into Bobby's eyes, "Help me!"

Kye's voice sounded above. "Grace! Grace!"

"I've got you," Bobby said.

His fingers manipulated her forearm as if fighting for a better hold. She slipped. A scream ripped from her throat.

"I've got you," he repeated even as she felt his grasp weaken. "Grace!"

Kye reached the edge and grasped at air just as she peeled away from Bobby and plummeted.

# 15

"Grace!" The cry ripped from Kye's throat as he watched her tumble head over heels down the escarpment. She landed in a heap too far away for him to see if she was seriously hurt.

He leapt toward the edge as Bobby scrambled to his feet. Like a professional linebacker, Bobby tackled Kye.

"What are you doing?" Kye pulled back his fisted hand and then let it fly, cracking Bobby in the jaw and stunning him. This offered just enough time for Kye to spin out of his grasp and break free.

He scrambled for the cliff edge. "Grace! Grace!"

Bobby yanked Kye back again. "Get a grip! Falling down after her isn't going to help. It'll just kill you too."

Kye cranked back his arm again and Bobby dropped his hold. He held up his hands in surrender. "We'll get her out, but we need to be smart about it."

Kye invaded Bobby's personal space, grabbed a fistful of shirt, and pulled him nose to nose. "We are not leaving here without her."

Bobby nodded. "We won't."

Kye pushed Bobby out of the way and scanned the bottom of the ravine. "Grace? Are you OK? Don't move."

A moan rose from her still form littered on the rocky bottom and he inwardly cheered that at least it meant she was conscious.

"I'm OK." She lifted her head and slowly stretched out her limbs, but she didn't sit up.

"Don't move!" he iterated. "I'm coming down."

"I think I'm OK. Bruised, but OK." She pushed herself up.

Why couldn't that woman ever listen? He squinted, but he still couldn't see if she was badly hurt. Kye thrust his phone above his head in the hopes of better reception. He needed to call for help.

Nothing.

"Does your phone work?"

Bobby pulled it out. "No bars."

Kye's attention bounced between Bobby and Grace. "We are at least a fifteen-minute hike to the nearest storage shed with a two-way connected to Judy, and maybe only a little bit further than that from camp." He focused again on Grace who now stood favoring one leg. She cranked her neck back as if trying to focus her eyes on them.

He allowed himself a brief second to celebrate that she was able to stand upright.

"Would you please stop moving!" he yelled.

Bobby's lips twitched as if Grace's defiance amused him.

"I've gotta get down there."

"Fine, climb down. But how are you going to get her back up here?" Bobby pointed out the steep incline the return trip demanded.

Kye hung his hands around the back of his neck. "I don't know. I'll worry about that once I get to her and assess her injuries." Would Bobby try and stop him?

Bobby shrugged. "I'll go get help from camp."

Grace no longer stood at the base of the rock wall. She now hunched against it. Was she shivering? Crying?

Kye locked eyes with Bobby. "Hurry."

"I'll go the minute I see you're safely down there."

Kye picked his way between trees and

253

rocks as he controlled his five-minute descent to Grace. The drizzle transitioned into a steady, but gentle rain, slowing his progress. His stomach sickened at the memory of her body crashing through these branches and stones.

"Are you OK?" He stooped beside her, never so happy to see her scraped and beautiful face. He gently cupped her chin. Deep gashes on her forehead had already begun to clot. Blood dribbled from another gash peeking out from under the hem of her shorts. But what concerned him most was how she gingerly held one swollen wrist.

"I started to feel a bit dizzy standing." She moved as if she planned to get back up and he gently stopped her.

"Just sit for a minute." He peered into her eyes.

She blushed, seemingly misreading his motive.

Her pupils appeared equal in size. That was a good sign. "How many fingers am I holding?"

"Two."

"How's your head and neck?"

"How do you think?" she groused.

He grinned. Her fall didn't dampen her spirit.

"Can she climb up?" Bobby called down

from the top, his head barely visible from their position on the bottom.

"Not quickly."

"I'm going for help."

"No," Grace sprung to her feet, winced, and teetered.

Kye wrapped a supporting arm around her waist. "You can't climb out of here with that wrist."

"I'm fine." She pushed herself away. "I already told you that. You need to get to that meeting and convince them Camp Moshe is worth saving. You shouldn't have come down here after me."

Her words stabbed his heart. How could she think he wouldn't come for her? Did she really think so little of him?

She shouted up to Bobby, "Wait for Kye, he's coming with you."

"No, I'm not," Kye bellowed. He pounded his forehead as if she were dense. "What's wrong with you?" He warred between wanting to shake her and wanting to kiss her senseless. "Getting you help is more important than the meeting."

"Nothing is more important than saving Camp Moshe," she roared back. "If they don't hear your reasoning against selling the shares, they might sign the purchase order and lose what Uncle Carl never wanted to sell." She paced the base of the cliff with a slight limp and gazed at the lip of the trail. "Bobby? Bobby?"

Silence.

"He must have already left."

She leaned back against the wall and shut her eyes. Her tears blended with raindrops, watering down Kye's anger.

He leaned a shoulder against the wall beside her and brushed away her tear with the pad of his thumb. "It'll be OK. One thing at a time."

"But if I had listened when you expressed your concern, we wouldn't be down here. Now, you'll miss the meeting, I'll miss the BBQ. If we lose the camp, it'll be all my fault."

Kye cupped her chin with his hand and waited for her to look at him. "No one is more devoted to Camp Moshe than you. I love that about you. But you've got to stop carrying this burden alone. It's not your job to save this place."

"Because it's your job?" Her spirited words contrasted her waning strength.

"No, it's His." He pointed his index finger to the sky.

She pulled herself from his grasp and hugged her body. "Maybe God wants to work through me."

"Maybe," Kye conceded. "Or maybe His plan is more about trust. Teaching you to trust Him with what matters most."

She huffed but her pained gaze lingered on his. Kye's heart pounded. Would she finally hear him? Would she finally understand he was as committed as she was? He was just beginning to learn that there were some things only God could fix.

She blinked, and the moment was gone. "I gotta get back to camp. There must be a back way out of here."

Weariness pressed his heart. "Let me look you over first. Then we can follow that stream." He pointed to a nearby trickle of water flowing down the rock face and making a skinny trail through the woods. "It has to empty into the lake at some point."

She gave a curt nod and managed to physically submit to his examination but maintain an emotional distance.

He started with her good arm, running his fingers along the bones and pausing at her wrist to check her pulse. Her heartbeat raced. But considering how his own heart beat out of control whenever she was near, he didn't attribute that to her fall. His pride hoped it had more to do with his nearness, but it was more likely anger related.

Then what explained the faint red creeping up her neck?

He continued his examination with trembling fingers. She could have died believing he didn't care about her.

He wanted her to trust God with the camp, but could he heed his own advice and trust God with what mattered most to him? With Grace?

He saved her swollen wrist for last, gently examining it. She pressed her lips flat, enduring his touch without complaint. It was likely a sprain. He released her hand. "The good news is that nothing seems broken."

"What's the bad news?" she grumbled.

"Sprains can hurt just as much as a break." He took her injured hand again, ignoring the way her eyebrows spiked. He laid it across her chest and rested it on her shoulder above her heart. "We should keep it elevated as much as possible."

"Oh, OK."

Was it disappointment that flashed in her eyes?

"On a scale of one to ten, where is your pain?"

"Maybe a five?" Her pinched expression upgraded her number.

"We'll be slow moving if you want to follow that stream, or we can wait. Bobby is going to be at least forty minutes getting to camp and back, maybe more if the rain slows him down."

Forty minutes. What on earth would they talk about? Grace had spent the better part of the last two days avoiding him, focusing solely on campaigning for her BBQ. She'd done a remarkable job. He tried several times to tell her and offered to help, but she had shut him down every time.

She shivered. From the onset of shock, or her drenched clothing?

"You're cold. Let me fix that." He draped his arm around her shoulders and tugged her in. "Combining our body heat will help you warm up."

Yeah, body heat. That was the reason he wanted her close.

"Fix my chill like you fixed the camp?" Her soft words hardly registered.

So much for not knowing what to talk about.

His muscles tightened and his cheek twitched. "That's not fair. It's not my fault things went south with Tony."

She shuddered again and ignored his answer. "Let's walk." She shoved off.

"Hey!" he furrowed his brow. "The walls. There's nothing on them. How come we didn't notice that before now?"

Grace's jaw went slack. "You're right." She scanned the entire area. "Could Bobby have had the wrong spot?"

The perpetual knot in his stomach tightened. The whole thing seemed wrong from the start. "Something doesn't add up . . ."

Her quivering lips escalated to mildly chattering teeth. The dampness combined with her injuries and their sedentary wait equaled a bad combination.

He shifted gears. They could deal with Bobby later. Now, he had to get her out of here. "I think you're right about finding our own way out. We can't wait for Bobby. I'll miss my flight and you'll miss your fundraiser."

"Let's go."

He caught her elbow. "Do you mind if I pray first?"

Gratefulness filled her expression. They might not agree on everything, but they certainly agreed about who held it all in His hands. Why had he waited so long to suggest it?

He entwined their fingers and ignored the jolt of attraction. "Lord, we don't know what to do, or what is happening here, but You do. Please give Grace the strength she'll need to hike, and please show us the way out. And God, reveal the truth behind all the attacks on Camp Moshe."

Her eyes remained closed as he concluded his simple prayer. Her full lips echoed his amen. What would it be like to lean in . . . ?

He tugged his hands away. A kiss wouldn't solve anything. It would complicate it.

"It's this way." He pointed out the way.

She hesitated and looked up to the cliff edge. "What if Bobby comes back?"

"He'll figure out what we did. He's a smart guy. Besides, we can call him as soon as we get a signal."

He slipped an arm around her waist to help support her. She could probably walk on her own; he just wasn't ready to let her go yet.

They followed the stream through the woods. It disappeared into the rock near the mouth of a cave. "If my memory serves me right, this cave opens up on the other side near a trail with much easier hiking than the one we came in on."

She eyed the cave like some women eye insects.

"Really?" He couldn't suppress his chuckle. "After fighting off a bear, rock climbing, being thrown by a horse, and a fall down the escarpment, a hike through caves is your breaking point?"

She shot him a dirty look. "It's . . . icky.

And dark."

He stretched his hands out on either side. "Your call."

"The cave," she grumbled, stooping low to enter first.

His gentle laugh mingled with the sounds of trickling water.

"What, don't you have any fears, Mr. Fix-it?"

He had fears all right. The most pressing of which was not getting her help in time to properly set her wrist. But his biggest fear was being trapped in a marriage with a woman he couldn't please.

Not that he would tell Grace that.

The wind lessened, replaced by fast and heavy water droplets splashing onto the stone floor. He rubbed his arms to generate heat. She must be freezing. They tunneled deeper before gaining precious headroom. The walls spread out. Cracks in the formation let in slivers of light.

"We're almost there." In a way, he hated for their hike to end. He had Phoenix waiting, and it held little appeal. If only she'd give him a reason to stay, a reason to rethink his theories on women and dating.

They cleared the cave and he exhaled relief when familiar trail markings pointed the way back to camp.

"We did it." He grinned and held up a hand for a high five.

She smacked it with her good palm. "I never doubted you." Her sweet smile undid his resolve. He couldn't look away, couldn't imagine walking away. Not even for Phoenix.

He slid his hand under her chin and tipped up her face. "Grace?" He said it like a question.

She stilled.

For a breathless moment, everything faded.

She swayed in, water droplets glistening on her eyelashes.

He slid a gentle kiss over her lips, his mouth feathering across hers, and then pulled back. He hovered, welcoming her hot breath against his face, measuring her reaction.

She closed the distance between them.

His hand slid down to her waist and fit her body against his. He fully captured her mouth.

Her arms wound around his neck, her fingertips dancing along the neckline of his T-shirt, sending shivers down his spine when they grazed his flesh. She leaned into the embrace for a glorious second, before gently pulling back.

He reluctantly broke the kiss. But instead of letting her go, he tugged her close.

She rested her head on his shoulder and slipped her arms around his waist. It felt right.

He tucked her head under his chin. "I'm starting to feel like there might be more for me than just work."

She pulled back and looked at him through clouded eyes. She smiled a brief, seemingly regretful smile. "You know, every once in a while, God gives me a glimpse of what might come next . . . and the ache for it nearly breaks me."

He didn't understand. Why did she look so sad?

"Something or someone will remind me of Becky. Of how she can't get married. She'll never have kids. And how it's my fault." She disentangled their arms. "I'm sorry, Kye. Until I get my program on solid ground, until I make sure they didn't die in vain — work is all I have. It's all I can have."

Her words sliced through his hope. "You can't mean that."

"I have to." She stepped back and stumbled away.

Kye's breath came in gasps. Did he imagine their connection or was her kiss just a result of their precarious circumstances?

The door to his heart slammed like a jail cell. Maybe she wasn't so different from Annette after all.

He straightened. "Then let's get out of here and get you back to your program. The sooner we wrap this up, the sooner I can be on that plane to Phoenix."

He let her lead the way. The minute his phone had a strong signal, he tried calling Bobby, but there was no answer.

When they reached the fork in the road, he couldn't just leave things. He snagged her good hand. "Are you sure" — he halted, and then lost his nerve. No guy wanted to get shot down twice in less than an hour — "Are you sure you're OK?"

He wasn't asking about her injuries and she knew it.

"I'm sure." The words bubbled out in a sob, but after a moment she gained control. "I'm fine. I'm certain the wrist is just a sprain. Besides, you need to get to that meeting."

He forced a smile. "You'll make the BBQ if you hurry. The nurse should be there."

She palmed tears from her face. Raising her gaze to meet his, she lifted her hand and briefly touched his cheek.

His eyes dampened.

She blinked. "Hopefully, I'll see you after

Phoenix."

As she walked away, he couldn't help but feel she was walking out of his life for good.

# 16

Grace didn't understand. If she was on her way back to everything that mattered to her, why did she feel like she'd left something important behind?

She stabilized her wrist with her good hand and picked her way through the thinning woods, sighing with relief when Camp Moshe's beach came into view. Rolling gray clouds dripped rain and choppy waves lapped the shore. Volunteers fought against the wind ripping at the tent tops. Grace's heart plummeted. How could God let this happen?

Dark clouds shadowed the small, but faithful few who turned out for the event and now chased blowing napkins, paper plates, and beach chairs. Maybe it was time to accept defeat? She massaged her throbbing wrist.

Kye had said nothing was broken. Did a broken heart count?

Heat flooded her face as she remembered their kiss and how she had brazenly leaned into him. For that brief second, everything that was wrong slid into the right position. Even so, what must he think of her?

"Grace!" Jeremy waved from across the beach.

She lumbered toward him, stepping around washed-up driftwood and leaves. The wind whipped her ponytail and sand stung her legs. With Kye on a plane to Phoenix and the storm gusting away, her last shred of hope to save Camp Moshe was lost.

"Mom's been looking for you everywhere," Jeremy ran to meet her halfway. "Mom said you should move the party inside but figured she should ask you first."

"Grace, what should we do about the tent? It ripped." Kaleb held a shredded piece of canvas in his hands.

"Grace, the arts and crafts silent auction table is soaked. I'm afraid it may have ruined some of the donated items." Kate held out a saturated paper that might have once been a poster or painting.

Grace swayed.

Kaleb grabbed her elbows to keep her upright. "Are you OK?"

*Where are you, God? I can't do this any-*

*more. It's too much. It's too hard.*

Kye's words rushed back. Maybe she wasn't supposed to do this alone? Had she picked up a burden that God had never meant for her to carry alone?

She gave herself a shake, and pain shot through her wrist. "I hurt my wrist, but I'll be OK." She scanned the destroyed party scene. Kye was right. This never would have been enough to save the camp. She pushed the overwhelming thought aside and focused on the task at hand. "Yes, Jeremy, move the party inside. Kaleb, pack up the tent. We'll deal with the rip later." She shook her head at the drooping mess of items in Kate's hands. "Salvage what you can."

Kaleb headed to the tent, but Kate and Jeremy lingered.

"Where's Kye?" Jeremy looked behind her at the way she had come, as if he expected his hero to bound out from the woods and save the day.

"On his way to Phoenix." Too bad Jeremy's hero couldn't be her hero too. She had let Kye slip away like the damp sand slipping out from under her feet. But that didn't mean she needed to let the camp slip away as easily. She would go down fighting.

"Did you tell him?" The corners of Kate's mouth pulled into a frown.

"Tell him what?" She feigned ignorance.

Kate sighed and tugged Grace a few steps away. "Did you tell Kye how you really feel?"

"How do you —"

"Oh, Grace," Kate gently squeezed Grace's upper arm. "It was obvious to everyone." Kate's smile appeared sad. "It's also obvious that every time you start to feel happy, start to build yourself a life, you let fresh grief swallow you."

Kate was right. Guilt waited to strike the minute she inched forward past the hurt, past the death of her family.

"Being alone is not safer," Kate promised. "Just lonelier." Kate squeezed her good hand as she backed away. "Something to think about."

Grace watched her friend dash to the arts and crafts table. She turned toward Jeremy and forced a cheerful tone. "Jeremy, I need to find the nurse. Can you round up the plates and cutlery —"

"I can help with that." Bobby rested a hand on Jeremy's shoulder. "We can put everything away, can't we, Jer?" He nodded at Grace. "Good to see you upright and well."

"Bobby! I'm so glad to see you. Did Kye get a hold of you?" She didn't wait for an answer. "You took us to the wrong place.

There was nothing on the wall —"

The shrill of her phone interrupted.

Kye?

"What happened to your face?" Jeremy squinted at Bobby's shiner.

"Nothing," he grumbled.

Kye should be sitting on a runway waiting for take-off. Grace turned from the guys to answer. "Shouldn't you be on a plane right now?" She checked her watch. Maybe the storm delayed his flight?

"Where are you?" he asked.

A deep rumble charged the air and the smell of certain rain wafted.

"The beach, why?" Their phone connection crackled.

"It was . . . all along it. I . . . his uncle today. Uncle Carl . . . tried to buy . . . years ago."

"What?" She plugged one ear and pressed the phone closer to the other. "I can't hear you. You're breaking up."

The wind whistled.

"Watch for . . . stay . . . coming." His panicked tone worried her more than the storm gaining strength.

The call disconnected.

"That was weird." She turned back to the guys, but Bobby and Jeremy were gone.

A crack of thunder split the air and startled the few remaining people on the beach.

"Where's Jeremy?" Grace's mom held a sunhat on her head as the quickening wind threatened to snatch it away.

"He left with Bobby to collect supplies from the food tent." She cupped her good hand around her mouth and yelled, "OK, everyone, we're taking the party inside!"

"They're not there." Her mom shouted to be heard over the chaos of people grabbing what they could and running to shelter. Paper napkins, plates, and plastic cutlery tumbled across the deserted food tent.

"They must have gone to get something else." But she had specifically asked them to collect the plates and cutlery. Where else could they have gone?

Feet pounded up behind her. A strong hand gripped her arm and spun her around.

"Ow!" She pulled her bad wrist against her body and then flinched at a sudden crack of thunder.

"It was Bobby," Kye panted, resting his hands on his knees. He glanced at her wrist. "Sorry about that."

She blinked against the fearsome pain surging through her chest. "What? What was Bobby?"

"Everything. He did it. All of it."

"All of what?" Ann interjected.

Grace staggered. Bobby?

"Jeremy!" She spun, scanning the beach-front. "He has Jeremy!"

"Who has Jeremy?" Ann's expression darkened.

In the distance, the boat shed door flapped against its hinges. It should be locked, especially in a storm.

Kye pointed.

She understood.

He grabbed her good hand, and they ran into the wind.

"That man who scammed Uncle Carl is related to Bobby," Kye shouted, panting hard. "He crashed the meeting. Pressured the board to sell shares. I made the connection and called you."

They darted into the deserted boatshed just as the rain began to fall.

"What did the board say?" She only half listened. How could he think she'd care about the meeting when her brother was missing?

"I don't know. I came to find you."

She stopped. "You came for me?"

"Of course." His brow puckered as if anything else was absurd.

He came to find her. He missed his flight to find her. Her anxiety lifted. She didn't need to do this alone.

Fishing gear, life jackets, and nets hung by hooks along the wall. The floating floor rocked beneath them, creaking and groaning with each wave. Only one camp motorboat bounced against the dock inside the shed. The second dock was empty.

Not good.

Dangerous scenarios of boating in an electrical storm flooded her mind.

"We'll find them," Kye promised, resting his hand on the small of her back.

"The lifeguard tower! We'll be able to see more from there." She took off for the tower, reaching the base as a streak of lightning split the sky. A motor roared in the distance. The missing camp boat skipped across the waves, Bobby at the wheel, and Jeremy waving his arms in distress.

"Jeremy!" she screamed.

Billowing clouds swirled into a darkening haze and created an eerie brownish-green tinge to the sky. The wind changed direction, raising gooseflesh.

Bright lightning flashed.

Grace squinted.

Jeremy struggled against Bobby for control of the wheel. The boat crested a wave, knocking Bobby backward. Jeremy grabbed the wheel and pointed them toward the beach.

Grace sobbed into Kye's shoulder, not wanting to watch, but unable to look away.

Bobby rose up behind Jeremy.

"Look out!" she screamed.

Bobby backhanded the boy and knocked him into the lake.

"Jeremy!" Ann's scream pierced the air a split second before Grace hit the water.

She powerfully cut through the short, uneven waves, adrenaline masking the pain shooting through her injured wrist. Her insides swirled like the sandy lake bottom at the repeat of history. Another day flooded her mind. Another sibling in the water. Another struggle.

A lump filled her airway. She gulped and gagged on a mouthful of lake.

The waves grew rougher the farther she swam. The sheer power of the lake tugged her off course. She lifted her head just enough to see. Where was he?

She pressed against the agony throbbing down her arm, sculled a bit with her good arm, and caught a flash of a red shirt.

Head down. Kick-glide. Kick-glide. She peeked again and a nasty wave slapped her face.

Kick . . . glide . . . kick . . . glide. She panted. Where was he?

Do not panic. Do. Not. Panic.

She'd lost her bearing.

Swim normal. That's what she'd tell a student.

Kick-glide. She caught her breath.

Kick, glide. She found her rhythm.

Kick, glide. She did a six kick and corrected her direction to the left.

She stole another look.

This time she didn't try to preserve strength. She stretched her head right out of the waves and spied him struggling to stay afloat using his water survival skills. She choked in relief. *Thank you, God!*

Her injured wrist made her stroke sloppy. She dragged her arm up and around. Over and over. Through the pain. Through the tears. She had to save him. This time she had to save him.

Was this what her dad had felt? How Becky felt? The sickening thought churned her gut. *Oh God, please help me!*

She pulled from her reserves and plowed ahead. Stroke, kick, glide. Stroke, kick, glide. She mentally repeated the steps over and over. Almost there. She reached out and grazed his skin as a huge wave shoved them both underwater, smashing them against submerged rocks. Jeremy went limp.

Her lungs burned. She reached for him again, but he slipped through her fingers.

She was not coming up for air without him! She fought the increasingly desperate urge to inhale, and her fingers collided with skin. She latched on.

She touched her toes on the sandy bottom and pushed up, finally breaking surface and gulping sweet oxygen. The current grabbed hold and slammed her into another rocky sandbar. She instinctively put her body between Jeremy and the rock.

She choked on a scream mixed with water and inhaled more lake. Gagging, she choked and broke surface again. The horizon tilted. Waves crashed over them. She thrust Jeremy toward the oxygen-rich air and cried out as something in her wrist snapped. She gagged again. She had to save him. She'd die before she gave up.

And in that moment she knew. This was why her father went in after Becky. This was the kind of love that risked everything. Not recklessly, but sacrificially.

She pushed Jeremy up again. Her lungs seared. She wasn't going to make it.

Then, Kye was there, pushing a rescue buoy toward them.

"Hang on, Grace!" Kye fumbled to maintain a hold on them both with one hand.

The water tossed a string of men with arms linked together back and forth. The waves rocked their fragile thread. They'd never get them both out alive.

She used what little she had left and pushed Jeremy toward Kye and the buoy. "Jeremy! Take Jeremy!"

"Grace —" His face contorted as he understood.

If they didn't get Jeremy out now, he would die. She pushed her brother with all her might and released him to Kye.

"Grace!" The line of men reeled Kye and Jeremy back toward shore. "Grace!" He struggled to release the buoy and it bobbed to the surface. His tears blended with the waves.

She lurched for the buoy, but a crash of water twisted her wrist and swallowed her scream. The buoy bobbed just out of reach.

Another wave rolled over her and knocked her sideways. Everything went black.

She had pushed herself away from him, forcing him to take Jeremy first. He knew what she was doing, and there was nothing he could do to stop her. His thundering heart drowned out the storm as the human chain of men pulled him and Jeremy to shore.

"Jeremy!" Her mother broke free of Graham's hold on her and sprinted across the beach.

The waves crashed around Kye as he staggered, cradling Jeremy in his arms.

She lunged toward her son, but Graham jerked her back.

"Let me go!" An animal-like wail exploded as she fought and scratched against Graham.

Kye positioned Jeremy on the sand, and the camp nurse and Debbie, Grace's assistant, dropped to his side. Satisfied he'd done all he could, he swung back toward the lake, plowing blindly toward the last spot he saw Grace.

Kaleb's fingers clamped on his forearm like a vice grip. Kye looked down the line of men risking their lives for Grace, exhaustion carved into their steely expressions but refusing to give up. Gratitude washed over him. He couldn't have done this alone.

Graham had a hold of Kaleb's forearm, Kaleb clamped onto Eric, and more men followed suit. The second human chain cautiously ventured into the lake, as lightning flashed and a thick bolt struck Moshe Island with a thunderous clap. They were running out of time.

Adrenaline overtook Kye's fatigue and he scanned the water for the buoy praying she had grabbed hold of it.

*Please, God, let us reach her in time.*

They trekked into the frothy water toward the red, bobbing rescue device. The swirling storm muddied the water and limited Kye's ability to see if Grace had a hold of it. They stretched as far as they could. What if the undercurrent swept her out further than they could reach?

He fought the wicked tug of the water. How could he know if they were in the same spot he'd left her? There was no marker, no way to be sure. He blindly swept underwater with his one available hand. Nothing there but the icy pull of death.

*Fight, Grace, fight,* he willed, straining to see through the torrential rain. He dove until his lungs screamed. *Help me, God, please!*

His heart leapt. His fingers brushed against something soft. He grabbed hold and yanked. The empty string connected to the buoy surfaced. Grace hadn't been able to hold onto it.

*No!*

Lightning lit the sky and Grace's body momentarily broke surface. A wave washed over her, submerging her again.

"There!" he shouted over the clap of thunder. He clawed his way toward her, snagged her leg underwater, and hauled her toward his body. Closed eyes and blue-lined lips shot fear through his veins.

"I've got her!" he roared. He supported her head on his shoulder and tucked his arm around her chest. The waves thrashed against them, trying to snatch her back. He tightened his hold as sheets of wet rolled over them.

The line dragged them to shore. One by one the men dropped to the sand as Debbie and another lifeguard snatched Grace from his grasp. Too exhausted to fight them, he dropped into Graham's outstretched arms.

"You did good, Son. You did good."

Debbie stretched Grace out on the sand. She checked her airway and breathing and began chest compressions. "One and two . . ." She pushed down powerfully on her chest forcing her heart to pump.

Kye dropped to his knees.

"Breath!" Her partner leaned over Grace, pinched her nose, and exhaled two life-giving breaths into her lungs.

"One and two and three and four and five and six and seven and eight and nine and ten."

"Breath!" The cycle repeated.

Over and over.

*Please, God. Please save her.*

He dragged his gaze from Grace's limp form to where Jeremy lay coughing and sputtering. His gaze collided with Grace's mother, and he couldn't camouflage his fear. She lunged their way.

Graham intercepted his wife. "You can't touch her," he croaked. "You can't touch her." He repeated the words until they sank through her layers of shock.

She stilled.

Graham released his grip only slightly. When he seemed satisfied she could remain calm, he let her go.

She sank to the ground near her still daughter and rocked back and forth quietly sobbing.

Kye crawled closer to Grace. He stroked her head and smoothed her damp hair off her face.

"I've got a pulse!" Debbie exclaimed.

Kye sobbed.

The rhythmic counting of rescue breathing continued. The nurse dropped down beside Debbie.

"Why isn't she breathing?" Kye cried.

The nursed raked her gaze over Grace.

Hot tears dripped onto Grace's hair, and he begged her to breathe. "Come on, baby, you can do it. Stay with us." Her chest rose and fell with each exhale of the lifeguard.

Sirens wailed in the distance. The storm raged. His ears roared. His vision narrowed and everything faded but Grace. He searched her face for signs of life. Nothing. But then . . . there it was: a shallow rise and fall of her chest. He choked with relief.

"She's breathing!"

"Keep breathing," he begged. "Just keep breathing. Keep breathing."

He looked at the nurse, desperate to deny what he saw in her face. Her pursed lips tipped down into a grim frown. Her voice dropped to a whisper and she seemed to pray. "Help her, God."

"Sir, you need to step back." A heavy hand fell on his shoulder.

Kye whipped around and growled a fierce challenge to anyone who dared try and separate him from Grace.

"Sir," the paramedic tried again.

During his stupor, the paramedics arrived. He looked about and took in the flashing red lights, the horror-stricken faces of their friends, and the shock in the eyes of her parents.

An insurmountable fear ripped through his body as they peeled him away from Grace. He might never see her alive again.

"Nooo!"

# 17

The ground beneath her rumbled. Bleeps and chaos fogged Grace's mind. Where was she?

Something pressed against her face. She tried to turn away but couldn't move her head. She snapped her eyes open.

"It's OK," a woman leaned over Grace, her words barely understandable. "It's an oxygen mask. You can't turn your head because your neck is temporarily stabilized."

Grace locked onto her sympathetic gaze.

"You're being loaded into the ambulance. We're taking you to the hospital. Do you remember what happened?" Her soothing lilt urged Grace to focus.

Pain seared her head. What happened? Her heavy eyelids fell shut in long blinks. Why couldn't she keep her eyes open?

The kind woman seemingly understood, but urged her to focus. "Stay with me, Grace. Your brother is in the ambulance ahead of us."

Jeremy! Grace jolted alert.

She fought the mask and agonizing daggers shot through her wrist. She couldn't force her mind past the blinding pain. White spots danced before her eyes. She was going to pass out.

"You need to lie still." The woman held down Grace's flailing arms. "Let's go," she shouted, banging on the ambulance wall.

Grace remembered Kye, seeing his face contorted with grief. She remembered pushing Jeremy toward him.

Did Jeremy die? A wail rose from her core.

The woman's words mumbled together. Another voice grumbled in return and more hands moved over her body. The woman fumbled with the I.V. line hooked into Grace's arm. She placed a cool hand on Grace's forehead. She leaned close and peered into Grace's eyes. "You need to remain still."

Grace drooped. One by one her muscles succumbed to whatever drug they must have injected into her I.V. line.

She moaned. Everything hurt so much. Losing her dad, her sister, and now Jeremy. If only the pain would go away. Just go away.

A solid beep filled the air.

Frantic voices faded as Grace distanced

herself from the pain. Her body jostled under busy hands.

But she no longer cared. She was tired of hurting.

The ambulance doors slammed with a frightening clank of finality. Kye jockeyed for a better view of Grace through the back window. His throat constricted at the rigid neck collar snapped around her neck. The paramedic's hands flew over the equipment and the machines beeped and whirred monitoring her heart rate. A medic pressed an oxygen mask to her face, and another prepared an injection.

"I'll follow in my car," he said to Graham, as Graham climbed into the ambulance's passenger seat. Ann had already left in the first ambulance with Jeremy.

Kye raised a hand to touch the back window just as the ambulance roared to life. The paramedics pulled away, taking Grace with them.

He raced for his car and collapsed into the front seat cradling his head in his hands. *Why, God?* His internal wails synced with the blaring emergency siren. His heart cried out to the One he instinctively knew had the power to change things . . . but sometimes He didn't.

"Excuse me, Mr. Campton?" Officer Ryley rapped on his window. "Can we ask you a few questions?"

Kye cracked the window and rain splattered inside. "Now's not a good time. I'm headed to the hospital. You are welcome to speak with me there."

"We'd really like to do this now —"

"Look Officer, I know you're just doing your job, but unless you plan to arrest me, I'm going to the hospital." He started the engine.

Ryley studied Kye for a brief second and then slipped his card through the window. "Call me the minute you have a chance."

Kye snatched the card and tossed it on the seat beside him. "Trust me. I'll do whatever I can to help you get this guy."

He pulled onto the road, a good few minutes behind the ambulance, and fought the temptation to make up the lost time. *Please God, save her.*

As he careened around a slippery corner, a familiar flash near the edge of the woods caught his eye.

It couldn't be . . .

He hit the brakes. The back end fishtailed, but he managed to pull to the side of the road without incident.

The continuing rain made it hard to see,

but it had looked like a person — Bobby — slinking through the trees. He grabbed the cop's card from the passenger seat. He dialed the number as he got out of the car. "I think I found Bobby. He's headed south, following the highway on foot through the woods."

"We'll be there in five. Do not engage him."

Kye disconnected. There was no way he was letting this guy get away.

Bobby thrashed through the trees. Kye took off in pursuit, keeping pace with him, but running uphill to a parallel path that provided a better vantage point. Kye sprinted along the higher ground gaining the occasional glimpse through the thinning trees.

Sirens wailed. *Finally, the police.*

Bobby neared a section that would move their trails apart. It was now or never. Kye dove. He tackled Bobby to the ground and they rolled head over heels into the ditch. Pain shot up his shoulder.

Bobby rolled out from under him and snagged a stick as he jumped to his feet. He jabbed it at Kye.

Kye twisted to the side and moved into a crouch. "You're not getting away."

Bobby swiped the stick again.

Kye swung around and landed a powerful kick to his gut.

"Ooph!" Bobby dropped to the ground.

Kye pushed a knee into Bobby's back and jerked both of his hands behind his back. "You deserve more than this!"

He ripped off his belt and strapped Bobby's hands together. Then he hauled him to his feet and slammed him against a tree. "Why'd you do it?"

Bobby smiled a sickly, bloodied grin. "My uncle promised fast money if I shut the camp down. But you and that stupid lifeguard couldn't take a hint."

Kye tightened his grip on Bobby's collar and pressed in until his breath fell heavy on Bobby's face. It took all of his self-control to refrain from beating the life out of him. "Why?"

Silence.

Kye twisted harder and Bobby winced. "My uncle wanted to mine the land. When you wouldn't give up and close, we tried to buy a controlling share, but you shut that down too. If you would have minded your own business —"

"This camp is my business," he growled.

Bobby gave a hollow laugh. "Doesn't matter now. The gold is fake."

"Doesn't matter?" Grace was fighting for

her life. Jeremy nearly drowned and he says it doesn't matter? "If they die, you better hope you land in jail. It'll be the only safe place."

Bobby's eyes widened. "I wasn't going to hurt the kid. If he hadn't fought back, we'd be sitting pretty in a cabin waiting for his daddy to deliver a ransom. I only meant to knock him down, not overboard."

"Why?"

"Those thugs who jumped me, I owe them money. If I didn't pay by —"

"That's enough, Kye. We heard it all." Ryley shouted from behind them. "We'll take it from here." Ryley kept one hand on his holster and approached slowly with his other hand extended in front of him.

Kye shoved Bobby in Ryley's direction. "He's all yours."

Bobby wiped his bloodied lip on his shoulder. "I could charge you with assault!"

Kye took a step forward and Ryley's partner blocked his path. "Let it be."

Let it be? A seething anger like nothing he'd ever known shot through his veins.

The officers slapped proper cuffs on Bobby and led him to the cruiser.

Ryley called over his shoulder, "I have even more questions for you now. I'll see you later, at the hospital."

Kye adjusted the stiff fabric of his borrowed scrubs. It was either scrubs, or go home and change out of his muddy clothes. And there was no way he was leaving Grace.

He squeezed Grace's good hand. "Grace, I know you can hear me. You need to open your eyes." The other hand had been wrapped and set after x-rays confirmed she had broken her wrist in the water.

"Maybe you should get something to eat?" Tamera said from where she leaned against the doorframe. "You've been sitting there for hours."

"No thanks, Mom." He shook his head. "I want to be here when she wakes up."

"The doctor said it could be —"

"I know what the doctor said," he snapped. They had sedated Grace so they could treat her wounds and run tests. Now, they were waiting for her to rouse, but no one could say for certain when that would happen.

*If that would happen.*

His mother walked across the checkered linoleum floor, her shoes clicking with each step. She wrapped an arm around Kye's shoulder, seeming to understand his anger was not directed at her. "I'll get you something and bring it up. I won't be long."

He waited until her footsteps faded down the hall. Then he leaned forward and rested his head on the crisp, white sheet under Grace's arm. *God, show me what to do.*

He had always tackled life head on. Solved problems. Fixed things. But he couldn't make Grace open her eyes. He couldn't make her believe him when he said Jeremy was fine. He couldn't promise her that her program would run, and he couldn't give her anything to live for.

*Or could he?* He thought of their kiss and the way she had leaned into him for those brief and wonderful seconds.

"Come on, Grace, you have to try. I can't run Camp Moshe alone. And we make a pretty good team." The thought of life without her scared him more than anything else they'd endured these last few days. He slowly trailed a fingertip down her pale cheek and whispered, "Fight your way back to me."

She wasn't motivated. He got that. From her perspective she'd lost everything.

Everything except him.

But if pulling away from him and refocusing on her program after their shared kiss was any indication, he wasn't the prize she'd been fighting for. She wanted provincial recognition for her program. Or a holy pardon saying her self-imposed penance was complete.

"Kye, have you eaten anything?" Ann swooped in carrying an arrangement of flowers.

What was it about mothers needing to feed their children in times of crisis?

She set the flowers on the windowsill, momentarily fussing with the arrangement. She could fuss for hours and nothing would make the cold, sterile environment cheery.

"Do you think she can hear you?" Ann leaned forward and fluffed the pillow around Grace's head, pausing to brush a stray hair from her face. "Thank God this time is different, and I get to bring both my children home."

He didn't answer her. He suspected she wasn't really talking to him.

Ann took a deep breath, held it a minute, and then exhaled. She blinked hard, unable to camouflage her wet eyes. She sank into a stuffed chair that gave out a whoosh as she positioned herself for the long wait of waking. Grace's private room provided plenty of space for visitors, but nowhere to get comfortable.

"How's Jeremy?" He backhanded his

cheeks to erase any trace of dampness.

"Graham is with him, waiting for the doctor to sign his release."

She forced a brightness to her voice. "I hear they arrested Bobby."

Kye hid his smile and rotated his tender shoulder. "Yeah, I heard that too."

Ann pursed her lips. She lowered her voice, "Did he say why he did it?"

"Gold." Kye's mother stated from the doorway. Tamera carried a takeout bag from the cafeteria and a tray of coffees. She handed the food to her son. "Here's a sandwich and juice. Eat." She set the beverages on the small rolling table near the bed.

"Gold?" Ann echoed. Her mouth hung open in the most unladylike way.

Tamera picked up the remote control and clicked on the television. "It's all over the news." On the television screen, a local reporter held up a nugget of pyrite. Below him, the caption read, *Fool's Gold Fools Again*. Once the reporter had summarized the unbelievable details of Bobby's scheme and how his Uncle Frank had manipulated him, she clicked it off.

Grace's face remained unresponsive. Kye fisted the bed sheets. When would she rouse?

"Frank. Why does that name sound familiar?" Ann's brows pulled together.

"Frank Blackman. The ornery board member who gave me a hard time years ago." Uncle Carl walked in and embraced Ann engulfing her with his large frame. "How's our girl?"

"She'll be fine once she wakes up." Ann dug a tissue out of her purse and dabbed her eyes.

"Kye." Carl offered his hand. "From what I hear, we owe Jeremy and Grace's life to you. Thank you."

Kye swallowed the lump in his throat and shook his hand. "You're welcome, sir. But it wasn't just me out there." Kye knew better than anyone that he couldn't have done it without the other men wading into the water with him and the real thanks belonged to God.

Carl paused at the foot of Grace's bed and squeezed her toes. Quiet descended on the room.

"I used to tickle her toes when she was a girl. Remember how she belly-laughed?"

Ann smiled and tears rolled down her cheeks.

Carl whispered, "Come on, Grace. Laugh for Uncle Carl."

Kye held his breath.

Carl sighed and turned toward them. "Years ago, Frank made a splashy gesture about offering Camp Moshe the money needed to survive, but in private, he attached all sorts of strings to the offer. The newspapers made him out to be a community hero, but I never bought the story. I swayed the board to reject his offer, and that was the last we saw of Frank."

Ann shook her head. "All these years he thought the camp was sitting on gold? There's no gold here."

Kye couldn't help but smile at the dumbfounded look on her face. "We know that, but Frank didn't. He saw the thread of pyrite in the rocks, thought it looked like the real deal, but couldn't investigate without alerting Uncle Carl. He's been trying to control the property ever since. So when Bobby overheard Jeremy's claim to have found gold —"

"He panicked." Ann connected the dots.

"Yes. If word got out, the board would never sell."

A nurse poked her head in from the hall. "Excuse me, Mrs. Douglas, your son is asking for you."

Ann stood.

"We'll walk with you." Tamera linked arms with Ann and Uncle Carl, whispering something to them both. She turned back to Kye. "We'll leave you two alone for a bit."

Kye rolled his eyes. Even at a hospital bedside, his mother never stopped match-making.

Once the ladies left, he picked up Grace's hand again and stroked the backside of it. Maybe a little tough love would work. "Grace," he commanded. "Open your eyes. Enough is enough."

Nothing.

If tough love wouldn't work, maybe honest love would. He leaned forward until he hovered inches from her ear. "I'm not leaving you, so you might as well wake up." He paused and almost lost his nerve. Ever since he'd called off his wedding to Annette, he'd been afraid to risk his heart. But it was time to follow his own advice and stop playing it safe. "I love you, Grace. You need to know that I love you. I can't imagine Camp Moshe without you. I can't imagine another day without you. I passed on the Phoenix job. I want to be here — with you. But you have to wake up."

The machine at her bedside blipped. Kye dropped her hand. Did it work?

"Grace?"

She stirred and exhaled a soft moan.

He bolted to his feet. Should he call a nurse? Get a doctor? He spun on his heel but her hand snagged his.

She half-opened her eyes and looked at him sleepily.

His heart skipped. Did she hear his declaration? He sunk down onto the edge of her bed.

She licked dry lips. "Don't go," she said thickly.

"How do you feel?"

"Thirsty."

He grabbed a cup of ice chips and slipped one between her lips into her mouth, letting his fingertips linger along her jawline.

"Thanks." She sucked the chip and let her eyes drift closed.

Did she fall back asleep? He had to find a doctor but Grace's hand tightened in his. Her eyes opened slowly again, as if it sapped all her energy to do so. "So if Bobby had stuck around and heard it was fool's gold, all of this could have been avoided?"

She'd heard.

He waited for her to say something, anything, about his declaration of love.

Nothing.

"Ah, yeah, it was all Bobby," he stammered, needing to fill the awkward silence. Why wasn't she saying anything?

"Everything from the threatening notes to the fire in the kitchen. It was Bobby trying to discredit the camp. He even took advan-

298

tage of your little food spill the night of the barbeque. He'd been putting out bait for bears for weeks already. Then he called the insurance company to report our 'negligence'." Kye made air quotes with his fingers. "He thought if the camp closed, his uncle could swoop in with an offer to purchase and play hero."

"But he didn't count on the standing offer." Grace grimaced and slowly forced herself into a sitting position.

"Here, let me help." Kye slipped an arm around her waist, helped her sit up, and adjusted the pillow behind her back. "When Bobby heard about the standing offer, he went from trying to close the camp to convincing the board to sell shares. If he could buy enough shares and add them to his uncle's, they would gain the controlling majority."

"And if all the staff were buying up shares, no one would blink at him snagging a few extra." Her eyes clouded over. Was she remembering their struggle in the water?

He covered her hands with his, drawing her attention back to him. "But then you planned the BBQ and the crowdfunding page, which proved to be solid ideas. You were right. There are loads of local families who believe in Camp Moshe and all it stands for. Your crowdfunding page raised enough to give the board pause, and that was the final straw."

A nurse bustled into the room holding a clipboard. "Why hello, Sleeping Beauty. Nice to see you decided to join us." She glanced at Kye. "I need to check her. Can you step outside for a minute, please?"

He moved a few feet away, and the nurse drew the curtain around the bed.

"That's one Prince Charming you've got there. He hasn't left your side since we brought you in. I wouldn't mind waking up to him watching over me."

"He's my boss," Grace corrected.

Her words slammed the air from Kye's chest. That's how she saw him? As her boss?

After a fleeting sensation of defeat, a sudden grin split his face. It was time this risk-taker removed the safety harness from around his heart and proved to Grace once and for all that love was a chance worth taking.

And he knew just how to do that.

# 18

A glance in her compact mirror confirmed her fears. A reflection of tangled hair and bruises stared back at her. She grazed her fingertips over growing discoloration on her cheekbone and tipped her chin. She looked a mess, no matter what angle she used.

The curtains surrounding her bed swooshed aside. "I thought you might like some toiletries to clean up before your release." Her mother plunked a bag of items on the side table. "And maybe some help?"

Her expression contained such a mixture of hope and love that Grace smiled despite exhaustion. "I'd love some help, thanks."

Mom set the compact aside. "You don't need that." She pulled a paddle brush from the bag and positioned herself on the bed behind Grace.

She started working through the knots and softly humming.

"Mom? Was it all my fault?"

Ann paused in mid-stroke.

Grace's shoulders heaved as the dam burst. "If I hadn't been so pigheaded about my program, maybe none of this would have happened and we wouldn't have almost lost," she sucked in air, "almost lost, Jeremy like we did Becky and Dad."

Ann wrapped Grace in her arms like she used to when Grace was small. She palmed soothing circles on her back and rocked her back and forth. "This was not your fault. It was Bobby's." She tipped Grace's chin. Her tone was light. "And now that he's gone, we can focus on what matters. Recovery and saving your program."

Grace's eyes widened. Her mom had never supported Water Survival for Non-Swimmers.

"You won't be able to fulfill the grant qualifications with a broken wrist." Ann continued as if Grace's mouth wasn't gaping. "So the grant is out. But, those skills you teach helped save Jeremy's life. I'm convinced."

"Convinced of what?"

"That this program is needed. If your sister had had those skills, maybe things would have been different . . ." Her voice faded, and a far-off look washed over her expression.

Grace's eyes filled. "What are you saying, Mom?"

She patted Grace's hand. "That it's OK for you take the summer and heal. Debbie can take over your camp responsibilities, and you don't need to worry about the grant. Graham and I will personally back you when you're ready to launch a national campaign."

"You don't have to do . . ."

Ann squeezed her fingers. "Graham has always wanted to, but I had this crazy idea that if you never got funding, you'd give up and move onto something safer. But, I see how wrong that was." She stroked Grace's cheek with the back of her fingers, wincing when she reached the purple bruise. "Now, let's finish up. There's an eager young man waiting to see you." Ann smiled down at Grace with a gentleness Grace hadn't seen in years. "I like him, Grace. And your father would have too."

Grace's eyes welled at the mention of Dad. He had loved her and Becky enough to risk his life to save them. And all these years Uncle Carl had tried over and over to convince her that it wasn't a reckless decision. He had said her dad followed the Lord's example, and how a good father would give anything for his child — including His life on a cross. That's not reckless, but intentional, sacrificial, and driven by love.

Mom finished her hair and ensured Grace was comfortable before opening the door for Kye. "You'll see her home?" she asked.

"Within the hour," he promised.

"How are you?" Kye pulled up a chair to the bedside and set some papers on the table beside it. He scooped up her hand. He looked far more comfortable in his casual shorts and a white button down shirt than he did in yesterday's scrubs. "Do you remember much?"

She bounced her gaze to the ceiling. She remembered more than she was willing to admit. What if his profession of love was the fear talking? What if he regretted saying he would stick around? She needed to give him a graceful out. She owed him that. She forced a cheeky grin. "I remember you were supposed to be in Phoenix right now."

His eyes never left her face. "I couldn't leave you."

"What about your job?"

He shrugged, and a curious smile turned up the corners of his lips. "I find that I don't care about my job nearly as much as I did before."

Her breath caught.

"I quit." He looked rather pleased for a guy who had given up a high-powered, high-paying job on a whim.

"Why?" She hoped he couldn't hear the pounding in her chest.

He leaned in and rested his forearms on the bed, bringing them eye-to-eye. "When you pushed Jeremy to me, I knew what you were doing. And part of me wants to make you promise never to take that kind of risk again. But I can't."

"No?" Heat rushed her cheeks. She had had no problem asking him to tone down his risk-taking.

"No." he caressed her cheek so lightly she wasn't sure if he actually touched her. "Because some risks require a sacrifice worth making."

She frowned. Was he referring to his job?

He leaned in.

Her breath caught. He was going to kiss her.

He cupped the back of her neck with one hand and tugged her forward.

She closed her eyes, and his sweet exhalation washed over her face . . .

"Kye!"

Grace jerked back at Tamera's voice. His warm lips bypassed hers and pressed against her temple. He tipped his head and their foreheads touched. He sighed. "Yes, Mom?"

Grace chuckled. For a woman desperate to see him settled, his mother couldn't have chosen a worse time to barge in.

"I just wanted to see if Grace was OK. I'm sorry, I didn't mean . . ." She was beside herself for intruding.

Compassion surged. "It's OK," Grace said. She leaned against her pillow and resisted the urge to fan her face over the heat in Kye's eyes.

"Did you show her?" Tamera asked.

Grace perked. "Show me what?"

"This." Kye flipped over the papers he had sat down on the table and laid them on her lap.

The bar graph of numbers and tallies meant little to her. "What's this?"

He grinned. "Your crowdfunding page. The news picked up the story, interviewed Jeremy and Graham, and they both praised the survival skills learned in your program. They mentioned your choice to debut the program locally at Camp Moshe in an effort to save the camp from closure, and *bang* — it went viral."

She shook her head. These numbers couldn't be right . . .

"Grace." Kye laughed. "You did it."

"Did what exactly?" She still couldn't

process what it all meant. It couldn't be true.

"Kye arranged interviews of the locals giving testimony to what Camp Moshe meant to them. The news has been running stories all day!" Tamera gushed.

"What does this mean?" Grace didn't dare hope or breathe . . .

Kye wiped a tear from her cheek that she hadn't even realized had fallen. "It means you raised more than enough money to save Camp Moshe. So much that we won't have to raise camp prices. We'll be able to keep this place affordable for the kids who need it most."

The paper trembled in her hands. The sum total was more than she dared to dream possible. Tears smeared the ink on the page.

Kye's mom slipped out and tugged the curtain closed behind her. The door clicked shut.

Kye suddenly seemed unsure how to handle her mini-meltdown. "Do you need a nurse?"

"Don't." She laid a hand on his arm.

"Don't what?"

"Don't go until you've kissed me again."

A slow smile inched across his face. He settled onto the edge of the bed and the mattress groaned. He stroked her hair with the back of his fingers, and then grazed them down her cheek. He gently cupped her face with his palms and fixed his piercing eyes on hers. "You don't need to tell me twice."

The bleeps and chaos cluttering the ward outside her curtain diminished as he leaned in. Everything faded and her eyes drifted shut. He feathered his lips so lightly against hers, she wasn't totally sure he'd kissed her until he pulled away. A soft sigh slipped from her mouth.

His distinct scent of rugged man made her feel safe. Grace waited for the familiar flood of guilt, but for the first time, it never came. Fresh tears filled her eyes.

"You're crying again?" He tipped his forehead against hers and traced the dampness with the tip of his finger. His eyelashes fluttered against her cheek. A teardrop splattered against the stiff sheets.

"Just happy."

"Well, if it makes you happy . . ." He chuckled and scooped her up in his arms.

"Kye!" she shrieked.

A nurse poked her head around the curtain. "Everything OK in here? Oh!" She backed out and fully closed the curtain.

Kye lowered her to her feet and tucked her into his arms. He rested his chin on the top of her head.

*A girl could get used to this.* She tipped her head back and examined his face. "What about your work?" He couldn't remain unemployed and hang around the camp forever. But as quick as the question came, it lifted. This was Kye, after all. A man with a plan.

His eyes stayed on her lips as though he thought about kissing her again. She hoped he would.

"Uncle Carl loves retirement, and it just happens that the board asked him to recommend a new director —"

He pressed a hand to her chest, just over her heart. No doubt he could feel it pounding. She covered it with her palm. "And he named me."

"What about adventure? Seeking the next thrill?"

He squeezed her fingers and tightened the arm around her waist. "We can have a lifetime of adventures together, if you'll have me."

She shivered as he moved his fingers to caress her earlobe and then lightly traced the line of her jaw before running the pad of his finger over her lips.

Who would have thought a sterile hospital room would become the most romantic place on earth? "I wouldn't have it any other way."

He cradled her face and she closed her eyes.

Nothing.

She peeked.

He waited, nose to nose, studying her.

"What are you doing?"

"I'm taking my time." He claimed her mouth with such gentleness it settled her fears. Her heart and future was safe with him.

# ABOUT THE AUTHOR

**Stacey Weeks** is the author of *The Builder's Reluctant Bride* (Pelican Book Group 2016) and *Glorious Surrender* (Women's Journey of Faith winner 2016). Stacey lives in Ontario with her husband and children where they serve in full-time ministry and homeschool their three children. Stacey loves to hear from her readers. Visit her website: www.staceyweeks.com